By Jessica Sorensen

For information:

jessicasorensen.com

Cover Design and Photography: Mae I Design

www.maeidesign.com

Untamed (Unbeautiful, #2)

ISBN: 978-1507680612

Chapter 1

A Dangerous Attraction

Ryler

Emery, Emery, Emery,

a song in my head,

stuck on repeat.

I don't know what's wrong with me.

I barely know her,

yet I can't stop thinking about her.

How her lips felt,

so hot and soft against mine.

How amazing she tasted,

like untouchable sunlight.

Emery, Emery, Emery

My attraction to her is dangerous.

Beautifully dangerous.

The kind of danger I don't necessarily mind,

yet I have to.

God, what I would give

for things to be easy,

for Emery to be the Emery I first met,

for her to be touchable,

instead of so far away,

even when she's sitting right across from me.

My hand stops moving across the page as I glance across the room at Emery sitting on a barstool, writing. We're supposed to be working together on a Creative Writing partner project that was assigned in class today. The instructions were to interview your partner and then write a poem about them. But since we hardly talk to each other, Emery and I silently decided to complete the project solo. Instead of writing about Emery, I ended up writing about my feelings for her.

"What's wrong?" Her soft, tentative voice interrupts my thoughts.

She's wearing a short pair of shorts that make her ass look fucking amazing every time she bends over and a thin-strapped tank top that shows off her bare shoulders. Her long, brown hair is curled and runs down her back. Her lips are luscious, and her gorgeous eyes are locked on me and filled with curiosity.

"Ryler, what's up?" She chews on her pen with her head tipped to the side. "You've been staring at me for, like, the last ten minutes. Do I have something on my face?" She self-consciously runs her fingers across her cheeks and forehead.

Another thing I've learned. For such a beautiful girl, Emery is extremely self-conscious.

I shake my head and check the time on the clock. Realizing how much time has drifted by since I started staring at her, I set my pen and notebook aside on the sofa and stretch my arms above my head.

"Sorry," I sign to her. "I've just got a lot on my mind and spaced out."

She studies me intently, and then her lips part, but she quickly closes her mouth, changing her mind on whatever she was about to say. She presses the tip of her pen to her notebook and starts scribbling in it again.

I want to tell her I'm sorry again. Sorry things turned out this way. Sorry for *everything*. Sorry that I took away the peace she felt whenever she spent time with me. But doing so could risk blowing my cover. So, instead I focus back on the paper.

I'm so sorry, sorry, sorry

that I'm a liar.

If I had my way,

I would tell you everything.

If I had my way,

I'd have you unconditionally.

But life isn't that simple.

8

Never has been.

We continue writing for what feels like an eternity, only stopping to take a break when Emery puts her pen down.

She stretches her arms above her head, arching her back. "I wish we had some music to listen to," she says through a yawn. "I've always wanted to listen to music while I'm writing."

I drop the pen onto my lap and flex my fingers, which are stiff from gripping the pen for the last three hours, then elevate my hands in front of me to sign, "You've never listened to music while you were writing?"

"No, I wasn't really allowed to listen to music back at home." She stares out the window, coiling a strand of her hair around her finger. "I probably should get an iPod or something, but I haven't really had the chance to since I've been under twenty-four hour surveillance."

I tap my foot on the floor, restless and unsure what to say since I'm part of the surveillance. Ever since Doc, her father, hired me to be her bodyguard, Emery has been cold and distant.

She turns back to me with a heavyhearted sigh. "Sorry."

"For what?"

"For complaining."

Always so apologetic. Always so afraid of saying the wrong thing. Emery has lived her life in fear, that much I'm sure of. I've seen firsthand what kind of a monster her father is, seen him kill someone with my own eyes. I've also picked up on little details of Emery's traumatic childhood through the few stories she's told me. That was before she found out I worked for her father, even though I technically don't. Really, I'm working as an informant for the police, have been for over eight months. My main goal is to find Doc's boss, Donny Elderman, one of the most dangerous mobster/drug lords in the country. To do so, I have to find the location of his main warehouse, which happens to be located in a hidden town no one seems to want to speak of.

Stale, the agent who gives me orders, is positive Emery knows where the town is and wants me to use her to find out its location. While I think he might be right, the idea of using Emery to get information makes me feel like an asshole. Doesn't really matter, though, since Emery barely speaks to me anymore.

She collects her pen again, and her hand flows across the paper, tracing letters with such passion. Whenever she writes, she looks so relaxed and into it, and I find it fascinating to watch. She's so calm, so at peace, so unlike the Emery I see during most of the day. She deserves to feel this all the time, and I wish I could make that possible for her.

A sudden idea clicks in my head. Setting my journal and pen down on the coffee table, I rise to my feet and walk toward the front door.

Her gaze flicks to me. "Where are you going?"

"I'll be right back," I sign, then open the door and slip out into the stairwell.

I trot down the flight of stairs to the second floor and push open the door to my apartment. Luke and Violet, my roommates, are cooking what smells like pasta; steam is flowing from the kitchen, and pots and pans cover the counters.

"Hey, you're just in time for dinner," Violet says from near the stove. She lifts the lid of a pan and peers inside. "Can I just say how great this smells?"

Luke opens the fridge door and grabs a soda. "Subtle way to compliment your cooking."

I envy their time together, but not because I have a thing for Violet. I just want to be free in life for once, to hang out without constantly looking over my shoulder or cringing every time my phone vibrates. I want to be able to curl up on the couch with Emery and watch a movie instead of staring at each other from across the room with distrust.

After kissing Violet again, Luke turns to me and pops the tab on the soda. "We're going to a concert after dinner if you want to hang out. There's no fancy bands or anything, just a little garage rock, but it could be fun."

Even though I'd give my left arm to go, I can't leave Emery for the night. I shake my head as I cross the living room, walking backwards. "I have to work on an assignment with Emery. I just came to get my record player."

Violet twists around and gives me a knowing look. Neither of them are aware that I'm an informant for the police. They think I live in Laramie to attend the University of Wyoming—that I came here to get a new start. To them, Emery is the strikingly beautiful girl who lives upstairs and has stolen my heart over the course of a month. What I would give for them to know my reality.

Want.

Want.

Want.

Please, just let me be free.

"You two sure have been spending a lot of time together," Violet remarks, collecting a spoon from the drawer.

"We're just friends." I squeeze past the two of them to get to the fridge and grab two beers, even though Emery isn't a big drinker. Honestly, with how stressed I am, I could drink both myself.

"That's what I used to say about Luke all the time." Violet flashes me a smirk. "And look how that turned out for me. Now I'm stuck with him." She winks at Luke who counters with a playful slap on her ass.

I shove the beers into the back pockets of my jeans then sign, "And that's my cue to leave."

I collect my record player from my room and a few of my favorite records and then head back into the living room with my arms full.

Luke and Violet are cuddling on the sofa with plates of spaghetti and watching TV.

"You sure you don't want to join us?" Violet asks as I maneuver the door open with one hand. "It'll be a lot of fun."

Part of me craves to sit down with them, be the third wheel, and go to the concert, just enjoy the goddamn night for once. But Doc would flip if he found out I left Emery's place too early, and honestly, I hate leaving her alone, not when someone has been sending her notes that could be interpreted as threats.

Shaking my head, I exit our apartment and climb the stairs to the third floor. When I make it back to Emery's place, she's moved from the stool to the sofa. She's still writing, her pen moving a million miles a minute as she stains the paper with ink.

14

When I shut the door, her head whips up. "Oh, my word, I didn't even hear you come in." Her eyes zone in on the record player in my arms, and for a fleeting instant, she perks up, her eyes sparkling with excitement. "You brought music?"

I nod, setting the player and records down on the coffee table. "I brought music and," I reach around to grab the two beers from my back pockets and put them down next to the record player, "drinks."

She sucks her bottom lip between her teeth, staring at the beers. "What do you plan on doing tonight?" Her voice is off-pitch, nervous, and her eyes are attentive. "Because it looks like you have more than homework planned."

I select a record and line it up on the player. "I have nothing else planned. I just thought this might help us relax a little."

Her attention zeroes in on me, and her brows elevate. "Did my father put you up to this? Did he tell you to try to get me to warm up to you so I'd trust you?"

I shake my head. "Your father has nothing to do with this." I position the needle in line with the record and twist on the power. "In fact, I'm not sure he'd appreciate me giving you beer and letting you listen to my music... I don't think he's a fan of punk rock."

"No, probably not. He likes old-school stuff, but never let my brother or me listen to it." Emery focuses on the player as the record spins, and "The Curse of Curves" by Cute Is What We Aim For flows through the speakers. She shuts her eyes and inhales deeply before opening her eyelids again. "I like this." She grabs one of the beers, pops the top, and slumps back in the sofa. "It's different... I like different."

"I know you do," I sign, dying to reach forward and press my lips to hers as I watch her mouth wrap around the top of the bottle.

She takes a swig, her face twisting from the taste. Silence encases us as our gazes fasten and smolder with heat. Finally, she tears her eyes away from mine and fixes her attention onto the beer bottle. She tips her head back and takes another long swallow before setting the bottle between her legs. "I don't want to work on the assignment anymore."

"But I thought you wanted to listen to music while you wrote?" I sink down on the edge of the coffee table. When my knees brush hers, her body tenses, yet she doesn't move her legs.

"What I want is to get out of this apartment," she utters softly, staring down the hallway with her brows knit.

I glance over my shoulder, curious at what she's looking at, but I find the hallway empty and dark.

Looking back at her, I raise my hands in front of me. "What do you want to do, then?"

She lifts her shoulders and shrugs, looking back at me. "Get out of this apartment. I haven't been allowed out of here except to go to school. I'm starting to go stir crazy."

"Emery, I don't think that's such a wise idea," I sign with reluctance. "Your father wants you to stay in until he can figure out who's leaving you those notes."

"No, he wants me locked in here, because he knows I'll go stir crazy and hopes it'll be enough to drive me home." She bends forward and snatches her pen and notebook from the table. "Never mind. Forget I asked." She practically stabs the pen through the paper as she begins to scribble words down again.

My lips desperately ache to surrender and give her what she wants. I want to give her everything she asks for, even if it means risking my cover. Or worse, my life. My attraction for her runs deep in my veins. Dangerously deep.

Chapter 2

Don't Let the Butterfly Out

Emery

Dying, dying, dying,

I feel like I'm dying

a slow death.

Each day, just a little bit more

tortured.

Just like I was back at home.

Only it's different this time.

Because I'm allowing myself to die.

Holding onto something that will never be.

Can never *be.*

Holding, holding, holding,

I need to let go.

Because in the end,

he was never really what I thought he could be.

Unable to stop myself, I peek up from my journal. Ryler is sitting on the opposite side of the sofa from me. He's been staring at me on and off ever since he rebutted my request to get out of the house. He stares at me every day. Ever since we found out one another's true identity, that's all we do—stare, stare, stare.

Right now, he has his head tipped down, absorbed in his writing. He looks like an untouchable piece of artwork so beautifully put together. So dangerously put together. He's undeniably gorgeous; with inky black hair hanging in his eyes and facial piercings and multiple tattoos decorating his skin. He turns me on in a way I didn't think was possible and is the exact opposite of Evan, my perfectly put together, pretty-boy ex-boyfriend.

I thought Ryler was different from everyone else in my life. Come to find out, he was part of the life I ran away from. Right in the center of it to be exact. He told me he didn't know who I was when we first met, that it was a coincidence we found each other. True or not, I can't seek freedom in him anymore, not when he's part of what restrained me. He's now my new bodyguard, a job title given to him by my father. In my eyes, Ryler is now an enemy. Every time he reminds me of who he really is, every time he follows my father's orders, I remind myself to stay away from him.

Easier said than done, since I can't get him out of my head. Whenever he looks at me, I try my best to ignore him, but my body has a built-in Ryler sensor. I'm hyperaware of every time he glances in my direction, and it makes our situation complicated.

I want him badly—there's no denying that—yet I can't have him. Not just because he's part of the world I've been trying to escape, either. If it were that simple, life would be pretty uncomplicated.

No, the complications between us are endless, ranging from Evan forcing his way back into my life to my father being super controlling. Plus, I'm wary if I can even trust Ryler.

Still, I always find myself stealing a glance at him whenever I get the opportunity. What I wouldn't give to be able to touch him again, kiss him, bask in his silence instead of fearing it. He makes it hard when he does stuff like bring his record player up simply because I stated I wanted to listen to music while we work.

Tears start to sting at my eyes as I remember the night I went down to Ryler's, right after Evan and I broke up over the phone. Every single breath, heartbeat, word exchanged felt magical. Light. Possibilities floated in the air like pixie dust. For once, my life seemed to be my own. But I was crazy to believe that would ever happen.

Crazy, crazy, crazy—the words are carved into my bones.

Around the fifth song, Ryler peers up at me from his writings. Our gazes collide and weld together, like they've done at least ten times tonight.

Dying, dying, dying. Feel how you pushing him away is killing you. You need to stop fighting what you want. I wish I could listen to my thoughts. Wish I could surrender to what my heart thinks it wants.

But the good girl I've been taught to be, the one I wish I could kill, keeps my lips sealed, and her attention focuses on the pages.

Slowly dying.

Dying.

Dying.

Dying.

Dying self-tortuously.

Ten minutes later, Ryler unexpectedly kills the music. The record makes a scratching noise before the room grows completely quiet. I angle my head back and look up at him standing directly in front of me with his arms crossed, his muscles flexed.

"What's wrong?" I rotate my wrist and check the time on my watch. Nine o'clock. Way earlier than he normally leaves. "Do you have to go somewhere?"

He sweeps fallen strands of his hair out of his eyes then signs, "*We're* going somewhere."

I frown. "Somewhere for my father?"

He shakes his head. "Actually, your father's out of town for a business meeting all weekend, so hopefully, he won't find out we went out tonight. In fact, he can't know we left the house tonight. You have to agree to this before we go out. I need you to promise me you'll be able to keep it a secret from him."

I don't know why, but I absentmindedly touch the tip of my finger to the silver butterfly pendant bracelet around my wrist that my mother gave me. She made me promise to never take it off, which I haven't. Keeping promises is one thing I've always been good at. Well, except for the pills I'm supposed to take. I haven't touched those since I moved out, but I tell my mother the opposite every time she brings them up.

"Okay, I promise." I rise to my feet. "Now, where are we going?"

"It's a surprise." He fishes his phone from his pocket, and his fingers tap the screen as he sends someone a text.

"Since when do you give me surprises?" I ask skeptically as I slip on my sandals.

"Since I remembered that I promised to give you a lot of firsts."

When the phone beeps, he reads the message, stuffs the phone back into his pocket, and then offers me the sexiest lopsided grin I've ever seen.

"How do you know I haven't done what we're doing tonight?"

"I don't know, but I have a hunch."

"Do I," I peer down at my cutoffs and tank top— definitely not the attire I normally wear when going outdoors, "need to change?"

He waves me off. "Nah. Where we're going, you'll fit right in." He offers me his hand.

He's being extremely sweet right now, and I find myself craving to lace my fingers through his. But then I remember how he's been sweet since I first met him, yet has been working for my father the entire time, and my walls go right back up.

I need to protect myself, so instead of taking his hand, I fetch my wallet from the counter then wrap my arms around myself. "So, when do I get to find out where we're going?"

My rejection causes him to frown. "When we get there. I want it to be a surprise."

"That's putting a lot of trust in you, isn't it?"

"You don't trust me?"

A small part of me does trust him; the part that remembers what it felt like to kiss him in his room, a kiss he allowed me to lead, something no one has ever let me do. But a bigger part of me remembers how he showed up on my doorstep with my father.

"I'm not sure," I reply honestly.

He nods then opens the door and steps out into the stairwell. I give one final glance over my shoulder toward the hallway where my brother Ellis is standing, nodding his head in approval.

I've been seeing Ellis more frequently as the pills slowly clear out of my system. My mind has become sharper, clearer, and I've dove head-on into a world full of what I think might be hallucinations. Despite the fact that I want to believe my parents wrongfully medicated me with pills for psychosis, it's difficult to deny the truth when it's standing in front of me in all its maddening form.

Like always, Ellis never gets close enough for me to reach out and see if he's just an illusion. Illusion or not, he resembles the real him to the point that it's almost painful; dark hair, the same eyes as me, tall, with pain continuously haunting his expression.

I want to speak to him—I usually do—but with Ryler here, watching my every move, it would be difficult to have a conversation with something that doesn't really exist.

"Go", Ellis mouths, motioning me to leave, *"just be careful."* His gaze falls to my wrist. "And don't let the butterfly out."

The pendant on my arm suddenly feels as though it weighs a hundred pounds. I'm supposed to wear the piece of jewelry all the time, per my mother's orders, but it seems imperative to remove it.

I lift my hand to examine the intricate metal, and the silver catches in the lighting above my head.

Blink.

Blink.

Blink.

They can see you.

My eyelids lift and open. The blinking has vanished, but an unsettling feeling still plagues me.

I need to take the bracelet off.

With trembling fingers, I unfasten the clasp, slip the bracelet off, and carefully place it on the coffee table. I massage my wrist, feeling as though I just removed a cuff, then exit the apartment, joining Ryler in the stairwell.

"You okay?" he signs as I lock up the door, concern written all over his face. "We don't have to go if you don't want to."

With a jerk on the doorknob, I double-check that the door is secured. "No, I want to go."

He nods, and then we descend the stairway toward the bottom floor. Strangely, without the bracelet on, my footsteps are lighter, the air is fresher, and my confidence is higher. I'm glad I decided to take the piece of jewelry off and wish I would have done so a long time ago.

Yes, I'm breaking rules, but I feel as though I've somehow sprouted wings and am soaring on my own.

Don't let the butterfly out indeed.

Chapter 3

A Dangerous Name

Ryler

As we make the twenty minute drive toward the club the concert is taking place at, I debate whether taking Emery out was a stupid plan or a fucking brilliant one. Perhaps both. Regardless, what's done is done. There's no going back now, despite my fear. There are going to be some major repercussions if Doc catches us, since he's given me strict orders not to let Emery out of her apartment at night unless he approves the trip.

Luke, Violet, Emery, and I are piled in my Dodge Challenger. Luke is driving since he's a recovering alcoholic and always assigns himself as the designated driver. He offered to drive his truck, but it's a single cab and has a habit of breaking down at least once a week.

"Your car's pretty badass," he remarks, revving up the engine at a stoplight.

"Yeah, it is. My dad tried to keep it when I moved out here," I sign to him from the passenger seat. "But I told him to go fuck himself since I'm the one who paid to get it fixed up."

"Good. Your dad's a fucking asshole." Luke hammers on the gas, and the tires spin as the car rips through the intersection.

"That he is," I agree, glancing behind me at Emery.

Violet is in the backseat with Emery, staring out the window. The two of them haven't uttered a word to each other, which isn't surprising. Violet is an intense girl and doesn't get along very well with others. Honestly, I think if the two of them gave each other a chance, they'd get along just fine. Both have had shitty lives, and it seems like enough to strike up a conversation.

"So, now can you tell me where we're going?" Emery asks, interrupting my thoughts.

Violet turns her head and gives me a look. "You haven't told her where we're going?"

I nonchalantly shrug. "I want to surprise her."

Violet's expression darkens with amusement. "How very boyfriendy of you."

I roll my eyes, but a trace of a smile reaches my lips. I move my hand to sign that we're just friends, but Emery beats me to the punch.

"We're just friends," she tells Violet. "And maybe not even that."

"What does that even mean?" Violet wonders, staring at Emery through the darkness of the cab. "You're like fuck buddies or something?"

Emery and I exchange a look, and then Emery quickly shakes her head. "No, not even close," she replies to Violet, then faces the window, letting her hair fall to the side of her face.

I think she might be blushing, and what I wouldn't give to be able to see it.

"Say whatever you want," Violet singsongs, crossing her arms and grinning. "But I don't believe you."

"You're trying to cause trouble," I sign to Violet, shooting her a warning look.

"I'm trying to put the truth out there," she signs back, discreetly nodding her head in Violet's direction. "You want her. You're just afraid for some reason."

"I'm not afraid." My hands move firmly in front of me.

"Yes, you are," she signs persistently. "You're afraid to have something you want because you're afraid of losing it. Trust me, I know these things because it's how I used to be."

She's so very wrong. If I could, I'd take Emery in my arms and kiss her until she became breathless, like I did a few times before shit hit the fan. Now, she barely looks at me.

Even if she did allow me to kiss her, Doc would kill me if he found out. According to him, Emery is meant to be with Evan, her once ex-boyfriend. The two of them have gotten back together over the last few weeks, even though it's apparent Emery loathes him. She cringes every time he touches her, frowns every time he looks at her, and tenses up every time he speaks to her.

"He's not afraid of himself," Emery abruptly says, apparently watching my and Violet's conversation. "He's afraid of me."

The cab grows awkwardly quiet, and I rotate back around in my seat and crank up some music. We make the rest of the drive in silence, and I get lost in my thoughts, wondering if that's what Emery thinks, that I'm afraid of her. Her father, yes. Her, no fucking way.

I need to tell her that's not true.

Ten minutes later, we're filing into the club. The music is deafening, but in the best way possible, vibrating the floor and my chest. The air smells like salt and alcohol, and the lighting is hypnotically low.

Emery pauses in the entryway, staring wide-eyed at the crowded dance floor. *"Holy shit,"* her lips mouth. Her gaze finds the stage where the singer is belting lyrics into the microphone, and she stares at him with her lips parted.

I lean toward her, grab her hand, and trace on her palm the words, "Is that a good shock or a bad one?"

She shivers from my touch. "Good shock." She peers over her shoulder and our lips nearly brush. It's the closest we've been to each other since Doc told her who I am. I want to eliminate the rest of the space between us, pull her closer, and devour her lips with mine. Fear stops me, though. "Thank you. I've never been to a concert before."

I step to the side of her to sign, "I didn't think so." Then I place my hand on the small of her back and steer her toward Violet and Luke who are standing at the bar in the midst of a clusterfuck of people.

"This band is crazy good!" Violet shouts over the music, then leans over the counter to flag the bartender down.

A middle-aged guy with a thick beard strolls over to Violet to take her order, unsubtly checking her out. Luke inches forward and drapes an arm around Violet, claiming her. The bartender decides to back off, but his gaze ends up on Emery, staring at her in a way that makes my blood boil.

Emery is an outrageously gorgeous girl who turns a lot of heads. Unlike how Luke did with Violet, I can't claim her because she's not mine.

"What do you guys want?" Violet hollers, flipping her red and black hair off her shoulder as she turns to us. "Unless you guys want to order for yourselves." She shoots me a teasing smirk, knowing Emery and I are underage and can't order our own drinks.

"Are we going big or going home?" I ask Violet, for once glad I have to sign because it's too damn loud to try to talk.

"Let's go big!" Violet shouts, fist pumping the air.

Luke shakes his head, stifling a laugh. "I'm going to have my hands full, aren't I?" He pulls her closer as she aims a devious grin at him.

I sign to Violet, "Shot of Jäger all around?" I glance back at Emery.

"I've never done shots except for that one time at your place," she admits, seeming embarrassed.

"We don't have to drink at all," I sign. "We can just listen to music and still have fun."

She slowly shakes her head, deciding. "No, I want to do this."

"Are you sure? Because we can just drink water, or Violet can get you a beer if you want."

"No," she replies firmly, straightening her stance. "I want to do shots."

When I still appear uncertain, Violet swats my arm. "Let the girl have fun, Ryler. Jesus." Then she turns back to the bartender and orders three shots of Jäger.

The bartender fills our order, and the three of us throw back the shots. We slam our glasses down on the bar, and I restrain a laugh when Emery shudders and chokes on a cough.

"You good?" I check.

She nods with her hand pressed to her chest.

Violet orders us another round and then another. Emery's confidence seems to grow with each shot as she sucks each one down easier.

"I feel so nice and warm inside," Emery remarks as she places the empty shot glass down on the bar.

Violet gives her a high five, and then they both bust up laughing, stumbling around as they work to catch their breaths. Like Emery, Violet isn't the biggest drinker.

"We're going to have our hands full tonight," Luke comments with amusement, leaning against the bar. "Aren't we?"

"Yeah, maybe." I look over at Violet and Emery who are giggling about something, as if they're best friends sharing a secret. I just hope Violet doesn't find out how we are really connected. The last thing I need is to have to explain to Luke and Violet what's going on.

"Let's go get a table," Violet declares after ordering another round of shots and paying the bartender. "Or should we go dance?"

Luke stuffs his hands into the pockets of his jeans and rocks back on his heels, looking utterly amused. "Whatever you want."

"Let's dance, then." She throws back the drink in her hand, sets the glass down, and then the two of them disappear in the crowd.

Emery's gaze slides to me. "What are we going to do?"

A thousand dirty thoughts cross my mind, but I can't act on any of them.

"We are going to finish our drinks." I raise the glass, and she clinks hers against mine.

I watch her as she lifts the brim to her lips, sucks the drink out, and then places the glass down. "It's starting to taste better." She wipes her lips with the back of her hand.

"That's because you've had four." I tip my head back, devour my drink, and then slip my free hand through Emery's. I leave the empty glass on the bar and tug her through the mob of intoxicated people.

"Where are we going?" Emery hollers over the sound of the music.

I turn my head toward her and mouth, *"To dance."* She instantly grows fidgety, so I pause. Releasing her hand, I sign, "Unless you don't want to."

She shakes her head as she skims over the rowdy people around us grinding against each other and crying out the lyrics to the song. "No… I want to." The florescent ceiling lights reflect in her pupils as her gaze resides back on me. "It's just that I've never gone to a club or anything. I went to prom, but," she shrugs, "Evan hates dancing. The only reason we went is because we were homecoming king and

39

queen." She sticks out her tongue and makes a gagging gesture—I'm pretty sure she only has the courage to do it because she's buzzed.

"I never went to any dances," *because I was in juvie,* "but I've been to a shitload of concerts, and I've learned one thing about dancing from all the experience."

"And what's that?"

"If you want to dance, dance. There's no judgment at these things, which makes them pretty awesome."

She smiles and then threads her fingers through mine. "Okay, let's dance, then."

I don't bother mentioning that dancing can be extremely sexy when done under the right circumstances— circumstances that usually include alcohol and sexual tension.

At first, Emery is cautious, keeping her distance from me as she rocks her hips to the music. I move with her. I've never really been into dancing, but I can rock out to a little garage rock any day. The longer the song goes on, the more into it she gets, until she finally spins around and presses her back against my chest. That's when the two of us de-

cide to start playing a dangerous game of Want But Can't Have. A very, very dangerous game that is really fucking tortuous to play yet impossible to give up.

Emery starts grinding her hips to the sultry beat of the song. With each movement, her ass brushes against my cock, making me go rock hard. I grip the curves of her hips and my hands unnecessarily slip underneath the bottom of her shirt. My fingers delve into her soft flesh, and I bite back a moan. Over the last couple of weeks, I've forgotten just how soft her skin is, how amazing she smells, how incredible she feels against me.

She shivers from my touch and presses closer, rolling her hips and driving my body absolutely mad. She repeats the movement over and over again, until finally, I damn near lose my mind.

Gripping her waist, I spin her around to face me. "I thought you didn't know how to dance?"

"No, I said I haven't been to a club before. I'm actually a very good dancer. So good I made the cheerleading squad."

"You're on the cheerleading squad?"

"No, I said I made it! I didn't want to be on it, though, so I didn't join. It reminds me too much of home where I'm…" She bites down on her lip to stop herself, but the alcohol must get the best of her because she ends up sputtering out, "of home where I'm always controlled." Her gaze drifts to the ceiling as if she's pondering something deeply.

My soul aches for her, but I don't say anything, knowing it'll only spook her more. I wait for her to bail out and leave me here, standing alone, like she normally does when she starts talking about her past, but the alcohol must overcome her fear, because she starts dancing again.

This time she goes wild, completely untamed. She flips her hair around and spins, even though there's barely any room to move. The throng seems to part for her, some watching her in awe, amazed by her flawless movements and striking perfection.

After about five minutes of me standing there, gaping at her, she seizes hold of my hands. "Come on, Ryler. Dance with me."

I chuckle lowly then join her, knowing that somehow I'm going to end up paying for it. But fuck it. If I'm going down, then I guess I might as well go down in flames.

I wrap my fingers around her arms and yank her closer until there isn't an ounce of space left between our sweaty bodies. Then I move with her, grinding against her, touching her body, and kissing her neck with every opportunity I get. She plays with the hair on the nape of my neck and nibbles on my earlobe a few times, eliciting a few groans that get swept away in the music.

If I had my way, we'd go on forever, but forever only lasts about an hour. Then we find a table to take a break, catch our breath, and drink more. Violet brings a double shot for each of us, then she and Luke wander back to the bar and end up chatting with their friends, Seth and Greyson, while waiting for more drinks.

Emery crosses her legs and fans her hand in front of her face. Her cheeks are flushed, her skin is damp with sweat, and her eyes are sparkling with excitement. "I haven't had this much fun since the last time we hung out."

"The last time we hung out?" My hands move as I cock my head to the side in confusion. "We hang out almost every day."

"I mean the last time we hung out when you were just you and I was just me." She spins the empty shot glass between her hands. "Before all the crazy stuff happened and life sucked again." She frowns as glass tips over, and she clumsily stands it upright again.

"Emery…" I'm uncertain what to sign to her. "You know we can still be friends, right?"

"No, we can't." She offers me the most emotionless smile I've ever seen. As beautiful as she is, I'll admit the emptiness behind the smile is sort of creepy. "Besides, you wouldn't want to be my friend if you really knew who I am." Her speech is starting to slur, which more than likely means she's not thinking before speaking. I raise my hands to cut her off, but she keeps mumbling. "I'm kind of crazy. Did you know that? Did my father tell you?"

I shake my head and scratch my neck uncomfortably. "He doesn't really talk about you that much."

"That's a really good thing." She props her elbow onto the table and rests her chin on her hand. "You'd hate me if he did."

"I could never hate you." Which is the truth. Wherever Emery comes from, I truly believe she's a good person, no matter what her father says about her.

"Yes, you could, if you knew who I am."

"Well, maybe you'd hate me if you knew who I am." Fuck, maybe I've had too much to drink as well.

She shakes her head lethargically. "No way. I could never hate anyone after all the things I've done. I'd be a hypocrite."

"Maybe I've done bad things, too," I sign. "Everyone probably has when you really think about it."

Her head slumps deeper into her hand. "What bad things have you done, Ryler? Do you… do you have blood on your hands?"

I pause, wondering if she somehow knows about my past. Knows about Ben. How could she, though? "Do you?"

"I don't know…" She yawns, her eyelids drooping. "You're really pretty."

I resist a laugh. "No, you're really pretty."

She wobbly shakes her head, sits up straight, and extends her arm across the table toward my hand, but ends up missing and tips over the glass again. This time she leaves it alone. "No, I'm being serious. You're like the prettiest guy I've ever seen." Her mouth droops to a frown. "No, I shouldn't say pretty. Evan's pretty. You're… like a gorgeous piece of art… with all your tattoos…" She finds my forearms and traces the lines of a skull tattoo. "And your piercings." She reaches for my brow to touch the metal loop in it, but misses and ends up poking me in the eye. "Sorry… Your eyes are so pretty, too. It looks like you're wearing eyeliner."

I bite back another laugh, finding her way too amusing right now. "You're making me sound really girly."

"No, you're not girly at all." Her expression is dead serious. "You're just so… sexy..." She stares at my mouth. "I really like your tongue piercing. In fact, it might be my favorite part about you. Well, looks-wise."

46

I have to bite down on my tongue just to keep myself from slamming my lips against hers. The way she's looking at me now, with lust in her eyes, is just plain agonizing not to act on.

Just when I think I can't take anymore of her kind words and desire-filled looks, she laces her fingers through my hair and plays with the strands. Like a magnet, my lips glide toward hers. I'm fully ready to suffer all the consequences just to feel her lips against mine again.

Right before our mouths connect, though, she suddenly pulls back, slapping her hand across her mouth. "I think I'm going to be sick." She springs from the chair and pushes her way to the bathroom.

My head flops back, and I release a deafening breath. Goddammit, what the hell was I thinking? Not only is she drunk, but I'd be in some serious shit with Doc if he ever found out. And the guy seems to know everything.

I send Violet in to check on Emery. Ten minutes later the two of them wander out. Emery looks tired; her eyelids are heavy, and her skin is pale.

"I need to go home," Emery says apologetically. "I'm so sorry, guys. I'm such a lightweight."

"I'm glad you are because I'm totally ready to get out of here," Luke replies, more to make Emery feel better than anything. "I have to get up early for work, anyway."

The four of us pile into the car. This time I sit in the backseat with Emery. She ends up falling asleep on my shoulder, her breath caressing my neck every time she exhales.

"She's not too bad," Violet remarks through a yawn. "We should hang out more often."

"I think that's the Jäger talking," Luke tells Violet, steering the car onto the main road.

The lampposts flicker inside the car as we pass them, and a song by Brand New plays from the stereo. Luke turns up the music a little, and I relax back in the seat.

Violet shakes her head and rests her head against the window. "No… way."

Luke and I both laugh as she passes out. Then he glances in the rearview mirror at me. "So, what's up with you two?"

I shrug, glancing down at Emery.

What's going on between us?

A dangerous game

that no one can really win.

The drive home feels short, but maybe that's because I'm enjoying having Emery cuddled up against me. By the time Luke parks my car, it's past two o'clock in the morning and the clouds have rolled in. He ends up having to carry Violet inside, and I do the same to Emery, taking her up to her apartment in my arms.

I put her in bed and pull the blankets over her. As I'm leaning back, she opens her eyes.

"Thank you, Ryler," she murmurs, then lifts her head and presses a soft kiss to my cheek.

"You're welcome," I sign in confusion. "But for what?"

"For taking me out and letting me have fun. No one has ever done that for me before."

"Well, thank you for going out with me."

"Would you…" she trails off. "Never mind."

"No, go ahead." I tuck a strand of her hair behind her ear. "I'm listening."

Her mouth opens as she yawns. "Would you lay by me until I fall asleep?"

I hesitate, but then she pouts out her lip, and I give in. Kicking off my boots, I climb into bed beside her, making sure to stay on the outside of the covers.

At first, we're both stiff, but then she unwinds and nuzzles against me. I can't even remember the last time I spent the night with a girl. I've somehow forgotten how much warmer the bed is when I'm not sleeping alone. Her body feels so inviting against mine, and every time she exhales, her breath tickles my cheek.

"Have you ever been in love before?" Emery murmurs as she sets her head on my shoulder and places a soft kiss on my flesh.

My body stiffens, but I think she's too drunk to notice. I shake my head.

"Really?" She yawns again, rotating her body and propping her chin up on my chest to look up at me. "I would have guessed you'd say yes."

I raise my hands, and she leans back to give me room to sign. "A few years ago I would have, but I learned my lesson over the last few years."

"Lesson over what?"

"That sometimes people think they're in love when they're really not."

"That's sad." Her lip juts out. "But I think it might be true for me."

"Really?"

She nods. "I once thought I was in love with Evan, but I think I was just seriously confused about love. I'm not sure I've ever felt it for anyone. At all."

"Me neither," I admit depressingly, but then force a stiff smile. "We still have time, though. We're still young."

"You might, but I'm going to end up marrying Evan." Her eyes snap wide as if she just realized the truth to her words.

"You don't have to marry him." My hands dance between us, speaking for me. "You have a choice."

"No, I don't." Her eyes well with tears, but she inhales, forcing them back. "Sorry, I shouldn't be talking to you about this."

"You can talk to me about anything," I assure her. "That's what I'm here for."

"Is it?" she whispers, then lowers herself onto the pillow. I figure she's upset with me again, but then she rolls to her side and rests her arm across my stomach.

I can't help myself. I pull her closer and breathe in the scent of her vanilla shampoo. She buries her face in my chest and then presses a kiss to the scar on my neck. My heart jolts to life, and I painfully realize something.

I'm not just going to go down in flames. I'm already on fire, and it's only a matter of time before I'm probably going to burn to death.

Chapter 4

A Visit from Evil

Emery

My head is pounding and every single one of my muscles throb. My mouth feels dry as sand, my throat burns like fire, and I reek of sweat. Sunlight streams through my window and onto the back of my neck, heating my skin. I'm so tired, too exhausted to open my eyes.

Ryler left sometime in the middle of the night, and the bed feels so empty without him. Last night was utterly amazing, although brief. Ryler was sweet, too, so sweet I forgot momentarily who he works for. If only he didn't work for my father. I'd ask him to run away with me. I don't even care how fairytale-ish that sounds. I want to get the hell out of this life, far, far, away where I'll never be found again. And if Ryler were with me, then my start wouldn't be so lonely and maybe easier to face.

"I'd open them if I were you," Ellis's voice fills my head, "because she's coming."

"Who's coming?" I murmur, burying my head into the pillow.

Hangover or not, I don't regret what happened last night. For once, I felt like I was being normal, drinking, dancing, and yes, even saying absurd things to Ryler about being pretty.

"Emery, I'm warning you," Ellis says in a panic. "Evil is coming. Get up before she takes you down."

My eyes snap open at the precise moment I hear the click of the lock from the front door. Only four people have a key to my place: me, Ryler, my father, and my…

"Emery," my mother calls out, the door clicking shut. "Where are you?"

I freeze, contemplating what to do next. *Maybe if I just stay put, she'll leave.*

"That's a stupid thought." Ellis appears in front of me. "And you're not a stupid girl." He waves his hand at me. "Now, hurry up and get the butterfly back on before she finds out."

54

"The butterfly?" I ask, and then it clicks. I push up from the bed, my gut churning as I remember taking the bracelet off last night. "Shit. Shit. Shit."

"Emery, I'm giving you five seconds to answer me and then I'm going to punish you," my mother says.

I can hear her rummaging around in my cupboards, probably looking for my pills. I hurry and run a comb through my hair, apply some lip-gloss, but then shudder when I glance at my reflection in the mirror. For my entire life, Mother has forced me to focus on my looks. Beauty on the outside is all that matters to her. Right now, I look like shit. Plain and simple. And she's going to be majorly pissed off.

"Good, let her be pissed," I mutter to myself. "I'm a grown woman. I shouldn't be afraid of my mother."

Ellis shakes his head with a frown etched in his face. "If you could remember what happened to me, you wouldn't be saying that."

I glance over my shoulder at him. "What do you mean?"

Before he can answer, my mother appears in the door-way. Ellis slinks back and vanishes into the wall.

"Who were you talking to?" my mother asks, glancing around my room suspiciously. "And what in God's name happened in here?" She pulls a face at the clothes on the floor, the unmade bed, and the trash bin overflowing with wrappers and soda cans. "This place is disgusting."

"I've been too busy with school and haven't had time to clean," I lie, running my fingers through my tangled hair.

Her eyes narrow on me. "You look like a disaster."

"Thank you," I reply dryly, my head pulsating. *I'm too hungover to deal with her shit.*

She points a finger at me and jabs me in the throat. "Don't you dare take that tone with me. Now get your ass into the living room. We have some things to discuss about last night."

About last night?

Swimming in a sea of confusion, I trail behind her, fol-lowing her into the living room.

She strides straight for the coffee table, shoves the record player out of the way, and snatches up my bracelet. "Now, would you like to tell me where you were last night?" She spins on her heels, facing me. "Or should I tell you?"

Her face is flawlessly smooth, even more than it was the last time I saw her, which means she probably had more work done. She's wearing a perfectly pressed blue pantsuit, and her hair is pulled back into a tight bun. Perfection. Perfection. Perfection. The word is written all over her, yet her perfection isn't real. It's just a façade, like everything else in my world. Each piece of my life is created to make people believe everything is perfect so no one will ever suspect how imperfect we really are.

"You should probably tell me," I dare reply, mainly because I'm not about to admit anything she doesn't know yet.

She huffs in irritation. "Don't play dumb with me, Emery. I know you went out last night with that loser guy your father has working for him."

"He's not a loser." Even though my voice is small, my words are daring. "He's actually nice."

"Nice." She says the word with such disdain as she wrinkles her nose. "He looks like trash."

Anger simmers under my skin. "He's not trash." My voice carries more confidence, and suddenly, I find words spilling from my lips. "He just looks different from what you're used to, and you think everyone who's different from you is trash or a loser or unworthy."

"Oh, he's unworthy of what he wants." She inches toward me, getting in my face.

I used to cower, but I discover an inner confidence I didn't know I possessed. Last night, I experienced so many new things, and if I want to keep going in that direction, I need to be brave and stand up to my mother. "He doesn't want anything. He's just doing his job."

"Exactly. You're just a job to him, so cut it out with the lovesick puppy act you've got going on."

"I'm not a lovesick puppy."

"Oh, Emery, what a stupid, naïve little girl you are. You have a stupid, little crush on a guy who isn't worthy of you when it comes to family and blood. Besides, he wouldn't want you if he really knew what you are."

"I'm not anything." My tone is shaky as rage thunders in my chest. "I'm just a person, nothing more, nothing less."

"You really think that?" she sneers. "You're so much more than what you think."

I swallow hard. "What do you mean?"

She leans in, whispering, "Ever wonder what those pills are for?"

I bite down on my lip to stop myself from saying, "I already know," and instead play dumb, shaking my head.

"Crazy," she whispers with a pleased grin. "You, daughter of mine, who is so perfectly put together, so flawless on the outside, are the most flawed on the inside. Your mind is flawed beyond fixing. Luckily for you, your father and I have managed to keep that a secret. And unlike your brother, who refused to hide his madness, for the most part, you've been a good girl."

"What's wrong with Ellis?" I tentatively ask, knowing more than likely the mention of my brother will set her off.

"What's not wrong with Ellis? The boy was born to rebel, to disobey, no matter how hard your father tried to beat the bad out of him. Ellis…" She shakes her head, but I detect a hint of remorse on her face. "Always clouding his mind with drugs. If he would have just obeyed, his life would have ended up so much better."

"How did his life end up?" I press for more details, despite how risky doing so is.

Her features instantly harden. Without warning, she raises her hand and slaps me hard. "Never mention your brother again." She shuffles back, trembling with fury, but quickly composes herself. "Now, get yourself together before you mess up the arrangement with Evan. If he finds out you're crazy, Emery—finds out you hear voices—he's not going to want you."

I touch my hand to my throbbing cheek and wince. "Maybe I don't want him."

A sharp, condescending laugh rings from her lips, making me feel about ten inches tall. "And what are you going to do as an alternative? Go be with the guy down-stairs?"

I carry her gaze, even though it goes against everything I was taught. "Maybe."

"Well, here's a little newsflash for you." She leans to-ward me again, her breath hot against my face. "He's not interested."

"How could you possibly know that?"

"How do you think I knew you went out with him last night?"

"I…" I have no idea what to say. There's no way Ryler would have told anyone, not when he was so adamant about keeping our outing a secret.

"He called your father and told him about it," my mother continues. "He even told your father that you agreed to keep it a secret from him. I have to say, Emery, your father and I are very disappointed in you—keeping secrets from us." Her gaze skims the wrappers and soda cans on the coffee table, the floor, and the counters. "The mess you live in, too." She pulls a face at a banana peel on the table. "What a disgrace you've become. Plus, you refuse to come home and clean up the mess you created." She pauses, as if waiting for me to agree to come home. When I don't say anything, she seizes my arm and hooks the bracelet around my wrist. Take that off again and you'll pay."

Blink.

Blink.

Blink.

The metal catches in the light again, and I swear to God I see a flash of red glimmering from the silver. When I blink, the light has faded, though.

With that, my mother turns, her heels clicking against the tile as she marches for the door. "Oh, and, Emery. Your father says if you keep receiving those letters, he's going to drag you home one way or another. It might just be time for you to face the inevitable."

After she leaves, I sink to the floor and rock back and forth. Tears fall from my eyes, and my breathing comes out ragged, her visit pushing me into depression.

"Don't let her get to you," Ellis says. "Be stronger than that."

I angle my chin up. He's standing near the sliding glass door that leads to the balcony, staring out the window with his back to me.

"She said I'm crazy."

"Maybe you are." He doesn't look at me as he tucks his hands into the pockets of his torn jeans. His messy appearance is so like him, Ellis, the rebel who never obeyed, who wouldn't comb his hair for my mother. "But that doesn't have to be a bad thing."

"How do you figure?" I sniffle, wiping the tears away with the back of my hand.

He glances at me, and I'm taken aback by the darkness haunting his eyes. "Emery, everyone is crazy in their own way if you really think about it. You don't have to let it own you. Be who you are and don't be ashamed of it."

His words strike my heart deep, making me pause to think. Could it really be that easy? Could I just live my life, accepting my crazy?

"What about Ryler?" I ask, pushing to my feet. "He told Father about last night. Why would he do that?"

Ellis shrugs, facing me. The sunlight hits his back, causing his body to appear as nothing more than a shadow. "Only he can answer that."

"So, I should ask him?"

"If you think you should."

"What do you think? Can I trust him?"

He smiles sadly. "Always asking the wrong questions."

I shake my head in frustration. "And you always answer everything in riddles. It makes it difficult to figure out what to ask."

"Perhaps, but life has never been easy for you or me. Life has been full of evil, and if you don't start asking the right questions, the evil is going to be the end of you." He fades in and out.

A split second later, I'm standing in the living room by myself with his words echoing in my head. *The evil is going to be the end of you.*

It sounds like an omen, that if I don't figure stuff out, my death may be coming. A death brought on by evil.

Chapter 5

The Truth Stings

Ryler

The morning after Emery and I go to the concert, I sneak out of her bed in the early hours of sunrise and head back to my place. It took a lot of effort to leave her warmth, and I missed it almost instantly. But I had to get home and put the wall back up between work and want. My job comes first and getting heavily involved with Emery is going to mess that up. We need to be friends somehow. I just can't figure out how.

I lie in my bed well into the afternoon, sporadically working on the assignment and wondering about Emery. Does she remember last night at all? If so, does that mean she won't be as cold and distant toward me anymore?

She's consuming my mind. Part of me wants to say to hell with my job and just let her consume me; run away

65

with her and never look back. The revelation is striking. The last time I had intense feelings like this was toward Aura, and that got me into a shit load of trouble.

I can't let myself get into that kind of trouble again.

Around two in the afternoon, I slip on a clean T-shirt along with my boots, then head upstairs to check on Emery like Doc has instructed me to do every day.

Halfway out the door, I receive a text from Doc.

Doc: If Emery asks, you told me that she went out last night. I know this sounds strange, but she needs to believe that you told me.

My heart skips a beat as I read the message. I pause in the stairwell, lighting up a cigarette as I try to think of how to respond.

Me: Okay.

I hesitate, not wanting to ask, but needing to know just how much trouble I'm going to be in.

Me: How did you know we went out?

Doc: I have my sources. Don't worry, Ryler, you're not in trouble. I know my daughter is hard to resist. I

know she's the one who instigated going out in the first place and you were just giving in to her.

Me: That's not quite how it happened.

Doc: You don't need to cover for her. I know the truth, Ryler.

Me: The truth is I took her out last night. It was all on me. I'm sorry.

Doc: I didn't text for a confession, Ryler. I simply texted you to make sure that if Emery asks how her mother and I found out about her going out last night— which trust me, she will ask—you are to tell her that you informed me because it's your job.

It feels like there's a threat hidden in his words, a do-or-else-you're-dead sort of thing. Not seeing another alternative, other than refuse and risk losing everything I've built over the last eight months, I text that I agree to do it. Then I put my phone away and finish off the cigarette while mentally cursing myself.

I kick the wall a few times, wishing I could scream until my lungs burst. God, I fucking hate this double life. I want out, but I have to finish first; otherwise, I'm walking back to a life almost as equally shitty as this one.

One of my neighbors walks out in the middle of my meltdown and gives me a horrified look. Unable to verbally apologize to him, I stop kicking the wall. Then I collect myself and drag my feet toward Emery's place.

It's mid-June, and the temperature is in the nineties. The sunlight blares down on me and heats up the fabric of my black pants and T-shirt as I ascend the stairs. For a moment, I wish I were a shorts and tank kind of guy, wish I were a different guy in a different life, but changing my clothes isn't going to make that possible.

When I reach Emery's door, I feel weighed down by what I'm about to do. I pause, mentally preparing myself, before using the key to get inside. I slam to a stop the second I step foot into the living room.

Emery is sitting on the sofa, her back rigid as a board, staring at the coffee table with her hands on her lap. There's nothing on the table, though, except for a half-eaten bag of chips.

I walk around so I can catch her eye. When she looks up at me, I move my hands, "Is everything okay?"

She shakes her head with her eyes fixed on me. "No, I don't think it is."

Something's off. I think about the text Doc just sent me and wonder if that's what might be behind her behavior.

"What's wrong?"

She stares at me hard, and I grow fidgety underneath her overpowering gaze. "My mother came to visit me," she says with her attention fixed on me.

My expression plummets. "Sorry. That sucks. I know how much you hate your visits with her."

"Do you?" She searches my eyes for something.

"Well, it always seems that way." I fiddle with the leather band on my wrist, wondering what the hell has caused her deep assessment of me. "I mean, I've seen her visit once and leave your house another time, and both times, it seemed like seeing her shook you up."

She bites down on her lip so forcefully the skin around her mouth turns white. "Did you tell my father we went out last night?" she sputters.

My body locks up and begs me not to answer, but fear of going against Doc burns in my throat, right beneath my scar. "I had to," my hands lie for me.

Instead of yelling at me, she folds her arms and sinks back in the sofa. "Okay." Her knee restlessly bounces up and down as her teeth sink deeper into her lip, drawing blood.

I round the coffee table and stand in her line of sight. "I had to. It's part of my job." My eyes plead with her to understand, but how could she? All she knows is that I work for her father, nothing more.

"Okay, I understand." She rises from the sofa and starts for the hallway, brushing past me. "I'm going to go work on the assignment."

I open my mouth, wishing I could call out to her, but not a single sound passes my lips. She shuts the door, disappearing into her room.

I grit my teeth, wanting to scream. But like always, the silence wins.

Over the next few days, Emery and I manage to finish our Creative Writing partner project without actually working together on it. We fall right back to our old routine of barely speaking, only it feels worse this time. After dancing, laughing, and getting drunk, then spending the night together, I was reminded of the spark between Emery and I, reminded of what I was missing out on over my choice to keep working as an informant.

When Wednesday rolls around, we drive to the University of Wyoming together, per her father's instructions. The drive is quiet and painful. Ten times I almost break down and tell her that it wasn't me, that I didn't betray her trust—that her father made me—but I'm starting to realize that the sole fact that I listened to her father in the first place will cause Emery to distrust me.

By the time we make it to the classroom, I'm sweating bullets from the stress. I've barely slept more than a few hours a night, spending a lot of time writing about my future, about my wants, about Emery in my journal.

Emery, Emery, Emery, she fills my head too much.

Consumes my thoughts.

I'm getting in too deep.

I need to get out,

but how?

How can that happen?

When I don't want it to end.

Don't want her to go.

Thankfully, being at school offers a distraction from the tension between Emery and me. We still have to sit by each other because Doc has made it pretty clear I'm not to let her out of my sight.

"I think we're going to fail the assignment," Emery mutters, frowning at her paper on the desk.

I jump from the sound of her voice. I think it might be the first time she's spoken to me since she asked me if I told her father.

I pop my knuckles then lift my hands in front of me. "We'll be fine," I sign when she looks up at me again. "You're a good writer." I offer her an encouraging smile.

I expect her to stop interacting with me, so she surprises me when she says, "You've never read anything I've written, so how could you possibly know that?"

Not entirely true, but I'm not about to declare that to her. When I first saw Emery, she'd thrown a handful of shredded journal pages out her window. I picked them up and caught a glimpse of a few of them. She wrote about her brother in such a way that I wondered if something tragic happened to him. After a crazy night with Doc, I learned that Emery's brother is in a coma because of a heroin overdose.

"True." I inch closer to her when the professor enters the classroom. Her body stiffens from my nearness, but I only inch closer, breathing in her scent. She smells fucking amazing, like vanilla and apples. "But I've seen how intense you get when you write. That much intensity has to come out pretty well on pages."

"Everyone's intense when they write," she utters quietly. "You are."

I offer her a lopsided smile that feels faker than my persona. "But I'm an excellent writer, so that just proves my point."

A trace of a smile touches her lips but then she starts biting her nails, a nervous habit of hers. "I don't want to be mad at you."

My heart squeezes in my chest like a vice grip. "Then don't be."

"I have to," she whispers, her eyes wide. "You told him we went out."

"I had to," I press back, silently begging: *please, please understand.* "I didn't have a choice."

"I'm starting to learn how wrong that statement is," she mutters with a frown. "We always have a choice. Sometimes the choices just suck."

I sigh heavily. "I don't know what else to say besides I'm sorry."

She shrugs, fiddling with the top button on her red tank top. "There's really not much else you can say. I get it. You had to do your job. I just don't know why you made such a big deal about me keeping our outing a secret when you were planning on telling him."

"I wasn't planning on telling him." I let the partial truth slip out, again wondering how the fuck Doc knew we went out. Does he have someone watching us? I haven't seen any suspicious cars around lately, but there are still lots of places for people to hide around our apartment complex. But if someone is watching us, why? "It just happened."

"I get it," she says sadly, folding her arms on top of her desk. "Your job is really important to you, and being on my father's good side is really important to your job."

You don't get it! You really don't. If I had my way, I'd pick you over working for your father. I'd pick it a thousand times over.

"How can I make it up to you?" I sign, my shoulders sagging. "Or is there not a way?"

She ponders my question, thrumming her finger against her lip. Then, her gaze falls to my paper, and she perks up a smidgeon. "Can I see what you wrote?"

I glance down at my paper then back at her. Most of the stuff I write is personal, and I usually don't share it with anyone unless I have to. This is a class project, though, which means the professor is going to read it. Besides, if I let her see it, then maybe I'll earn back a little of her trust.

"Sure." I hand the paper to her, but don't release it from my gasp when she grabs it. I mouth, *"Can I read yours, too?"*

She rolls her tongue in her mouth, her eyes drifting to the paper in front of her. "I guess so."

"No, never mind. You don't have to." *This is about me earning her trust, not the other way around.*

"No, it's okay. We should probably know what the other one wrote, anyway, since this is a partner project." Sighing, she picks up her paper and gives it to me.

I let go of mine, sit back in the chair, and begin to read what she wrote.

The guy I never knew,

a statue sitting across the room.

So flawlessly put together,

smooth imperfect pieces

that somehow create harmony.

His lips are the sanctuary to his soul,

never to utter the truth of the scars hidden inside,

begging to be free.

Or maybe not.

Perhaps they've sealed themselves up purposefully.

Silence.

Silence.

Silence.

*If you listen closely, you can hear the whisper of his
heart.*

Silence.

77

Silence.

Silence.

The rhythm is what I crave.

An addiction

I can no longer feed.

Silence.

Silence.

Silence.

I wonder what it would whisper if he were free.

There's more to it, but class starts before I can finish reading it. Emery snatches the paper from me and returns mine. Our fingers graze during the exchange, my skin burning as our gazes interlock.

Want, want, want, my heart beats the truth. *Want all you want, but can never have you. You and Emery were never meant to be.*

God, how the truth stings.

Chapter 6

Bloodstained Ribbons and Lace

Emery

I want to hate Ryler. I want to hate him because he chose my father over me, but hating him is proving to be a difficult task. With Ryler sitting beside me, class seems endless, especially after reading the paper he wrote for class.

Emery, Emery, Emery.

So beautiful.

Lips so kissable.

Eyes so haunting.

Soft skin that begs my fingers closer.

Untamed

Like a red rose,

she flourishes for the whole world.

But even though the rose thrives

through sunlight

and rain,

the rose is wilting.

Around the edges,

in desperate need of air.

Withering.

And the whole world simply watches.

As petal after petal falls

to the ground.

What I wouldn't give to pick each one up

and put them back.

Help her flourish again.

But I'm helpless,

bound by my silence.

His words somehow feel like an apology, but I'm not positive what he's apologizing for. For working for my father? For not being the person I thought he was? For telling my father he took me out the other night after he gave me one of the best nights of my life?

I try not to overanalyze what's going on between us too much, though. When it all comes down to it, Ryler still works for my father and he picked him over me. I shouldn't be surprised.

I spent the first couple of weeks pretending he didn't exist and should have stuck to it, yet I'm highly distracted during the class lecture, extremely aware of every time Ryler glances in my direction, every time he stares at me. I never imagined my time at school would be like this. I imagined freedom. The life I dreamed about during those late hours I spent strapped to my bed promised freedom. I'm starting to believe the dream is something that will never be. That the long road I wanted to jump off will always be

underneath me, leading me to my parents' future of me being married to Evan.

Maybe my mother is right. Perhaps fighting the inevitable is pointless. Perhaps, no matter what I do, I'm going
to end up right where I began.

"You want to drive my car home?" Ryler signs to me
after class is dismissed. He gathers his books and waits for
me to respond, appearing uneasy. "I have to go to work
right now, but I can walk home afterward so you don't have
to."

I shake my head as I collect my books from the desk.
"I'm fine. Evan's out there waiting for me, anyway." Liar.
Like poison on my tongue.

Shockingly, I feel awful for lying to him. I need to lie,
though, in order to get a few moments of peace and quiet,
some time to myself to decide what to do with my life.
Maybe I'll run. Maybe I'll stay. Maybe I'll cave. Maybe
I'll fight. I have no idea, but I need to figure out something,
because I can't keep going like this.

A walk home is all I have to attain some time for myself, because the moment I arrive at my apartment, Evan

will be there, ready to steal every ounce of my freedom and take it as his own. Wednesday is his day to visit me. *His* day to touch me. *His* day to claim me. At least that's what *he* claims.

A frown etches on Ryler's face as he lowers his head to read the screen of his phone. Then, he puts the phone away and signs, "I didn't know you were meeting... Evan."

Awkward silence envelopes us. I once told Ryler that Evan and I broke up—and we had—but Evan being Evan retracted the break up for me, and my father jumped right in. Now, I'm stuck dating Evan, even though I loathe him.

"Hey, are you okay?" Ryler stops in the doorway, blocking my way out. "You look upset… is it because of me telling your father? Because I seriously want to make it up to you, Emery. Just tell me what I can do."

"It's not that. Everything's fine." I smash my lips together and suck in a breath. "I should get going, though. Evan hates waiting."

Before he can say anything, I hug my books to my chest, squeeze around him, and hurry down the lonely hallway. It's midterm of the summer semester, and most students are at home, taking a break from school. Me, I took summer classes to get a head start—a new start.

Run, run, run to someplace new, someplace you can get a new start. What's stopping you?

I keep my head down as I exit the main entrance of the building and begin the short walk home. The sunlight beams down on the back of my neck and a warm breeze dances through my hair as I pass people and cross the street. By the time I make it to my apartment, my hair is a tangled mess, and my makeup is smeared from the few tears that have escaped my eyes. I kick off my shoes in the foyer and wander into the bathroom.

Staring in the mirror hanging on the wall, I admire my messy appearance.

Knock. Knock. Knock.

I squeeze my eyes shut at the sound. I know who it is without having to answer it. Evan is never late.

I glance at my reflection in the mirror one last time before heading for the front door. If I were the girl my mother raised, I'd wash my face and comb my hair, but I'm entering a dangerous rebellion.

She said I'm crazy, so let them think I'm crazy.

When I open the door and see no one is there, my heart misses a beat. I poke my head out the door and glance up and down then to the right at the parking lot. No one is around except for Violet. She's standing in front of an old truck, the long locks of her red and black hair blowing in the wind. The hood of the truck is up, and it looks like she might be checking the oil.

I scratch my head. Could she be the one who knocked? We did have a strange drunken moment where we got along and laughed together. But why knock and run?

I dare step outside and open my mouth to call out to her to see if maybe she saw someone leaving my apartment. But then my bare foot brushes against paper and my jaw snaps shut as my gaze drops to the ground. A single, white envelope wrapped in a red ribbon is resting on the mat.

"Not another one." I stare at the envelope for a few moments then bend over and scoop it up. Pressing it to my chest, I glance over at Violet, who's still working on the truck, one more time then duck back into my place.

86

I lock the door then lift the envelope from my chest and unlace the ribbon. But I pause as a warm, red substance stains my fingers. Blood. The ribbon is soaked with blood. I glance down at my shirt. Right above my heart, the lacy fabric is stained red.

My fingers tremble. "Oh, my God, whose blood is this?"

Not knowing any other way to get an answer, I rip open the envelope and shake the piece of paper out.

We know what you did.

I drop the envelope to the ground and jump back. My back slams against the door, and my knees buckle out from under me. *We know what you did.*

Blood on my hands. Blood on my hands. Someone knows what I did.

Tears pour from my eyes as I snatch up the piece of paper and envelope, tear them up, and throw them in the trash bin. Then I sprint back to the bathroom, strip my clothes off, hop into the shower, and scrub my skin under hot water. When I'm finished, I still feel dirty, but my tears have dried.

Wrapping a towel around myself, I leave the bathroom with a trail of steam following me. I veer right toward my bedroom, but grind to a halt when I hear my name called out.

"Emery, where do you think you're going?" Evan's voice floats from the living room and causes the hairs on the back of my neck to stand on end. "You've already kept me waiting too long."

I pull the towel closer to my body. "Sorry, I had to shower."

I hear him moving down the hallway toward me, and I squeeze my eyes shut. My body stiffens when I feel the heat of him sink into my skin. Moments later, his lips brush the back of my neck.

"You and I need to talk," he whispers, rubbing his hips against me, "about you moving in with me."

I lift my eyelids and stare at the end of the hallway, envisioning me opening the window and flying out into the world.

What would it be like to have wings?

To have such freedom to fly away

and disappear into the sky.

Fly away. Fly away high.

Fly away and never look back.

Soar through the freedom of air.

"I told you I'm not ready for that." My voice sounds as empty as my heart. Any amount of peace I felt crumbles.

Fly away, fly away, fly away.

Or allow yourself to slowly die.

Evan's fingers curl around my upper arms. "I think I can change your mind. In fact, I promise I can." His fingernails stab into my flesh as he shoves me toward my bedroom.

As I stumble onto my bed, he starts to make good on his promise, and shoves his tongue down my throat. We don't have sex, but only because he has to rush away for some sort of business meeting. Still, with each touch of his hands, another petal on that rose Ryler wrote about withers and falls to the ground. But he never shows to pick it up.

Chapter 7

Eyes, Eyes Everywhere

Ryler

After class, I meet Brooks, the other informant I've been working with for about three to four weeks now, at the Writing Center. He's sitting at the table, reading a book, and doesn't see me walk in. He always wears a baseball cap to keep himself hidden better, so I instantly notice his hat is missing today.

"Where's your hat?" I mouth, dropping my books onto the table in front of him.

He jumps from the sound of my books hitting the table then shrugs, seeming nervous as he yanks his hands through his blond hair. "I must have forgotten it today.

"You okay?" I mouth, pulling out a seat.

"Yep, fine," he answers.

90

Strange, but I don't think much of it until later.

We spend about an hour helping out students who wander in and out of the room, then we take a break. We chat a little bit about classes and dumb shit before we start talking about "work" related stuff.

"I'm starting to wonder if the warehouse is a myth," Brook says about ten minutes into our break.

Over the last few weeks of working with Brooks, he's been hardcore determined to take Donny Elderman down. Between him forgetting his hat and his declaration about the warehouse being a myth, red flags are popping up left and right.

My gaze skims over the bookshelves, the computer labs, and then the windows to our right. Nothing seems out of the ordinary. The area is as mellow as it usually is.

Leaning over in the chair, I grab my notebook from my bag to write down a response, since Brooks doesn't under-stand sign language well.

Really? Why? He has warehouses in Vegas. I've seen them myself. I slide the notebook across the table to him.

He picks it up and reads it over. "Yeah, but those are different from the warehouse everyone wants to find. The alleged hideout for Donny Elderman, where all his dirty stuff goes down. The ones in Vegas are basically just places to gamble and whorehouses." He shrugs and slumps back in the chair. "The one that everyone whispers of—the hideout—is… I don't know… I just don't think it's possible for an entire town full of corruption to be so far off the radar from everyone."

Off the radar is an understatement. Over the last couple of weeks, Detective Stale has spent hours searching for the town, even using satellite images to try to get a location. But he's come up with nothing, so either Brooks is correct and the place doesn't exist, or…

Maybe he's paid off people, I scribble down.

By *he,* I mean Donny Elderman, but I never jot his name down. If I did, I risk the chance of the paper falling into the wrong hands.

Brooks leans over the table, reads what I wrote, and then sinks back in the chair. "Do you know how many people he'd have to pay off to keep an entire town under the radar?"

I collect the pen again, thinking, *Yeah, but if anyone could do it, it'd be Elderman.* I don't write that down, though, choosing my words carefully. I rub my hand over my face and then press the tip of the pen to the paper. *I've heard detailed, gory stories of the things that happened down in this warehouse, man. I don't see why people would just make it up.*

"People make shit up all the time. It's how legends are created and how myths get turned into wild stories that people believe." He scratches at his wrist, and I notice a small, fresh cut.

Eyeing the scratch, I mouth, *"What happened?"*

Shaking his head, he yanks his sleeve down. "Nothing. I just cut myself on a stupid nail while I was helping my father in the shop."

My brows furrow as I mouth, *"Shop?"* What the hell? I've never heard of this shop before, and Brooks rarely helps his father due to the fact that he blames him for his brother's death.

Brooks shakes his head again and gives me a pressing look, begging me to understand something he can't say.

I resist the overwhelming urge to look around the room again, and instead scribble, *Are you okay, man?* I shove the paper across the table.

"I'm fine," he replies, then scoots the chair away from the table. He slings his bag over his shoulder and heads for the door. "I have to go. I'll see you later."

He still has another hour left of his shift. Something's definitely wrong.

As I start to stand up to chase after him, he turns around and mouths, *"Don't. They're watching me."*

Even though I desperately want to run after him and force him to tell me who *they* are, I make myself stay put. If Brooks is being watched, then I'm guessing I probably am, too. No wonder Doc knew I snuck Emery out last weekend.

I pick up the pen and write for the rest of my break, pretending everything's okay when it's not. Pretending I'm not desperate to get the fuck out of here and text Stale.

They're watching.

But who?

The Devil himself?

Or his allies?

Eyes, eyes everywhere,

hiding in the dark,

always watching

every move I make.

Nothing belongs to me

anymore.

Just like my voice.

Gone forever.

God, please, someone just help me get out.

Get out.

Get out.

Get out.

I want to be free.

For the first time in my life,

I just want to be me.

Whoever that is.

Run.

I want to run away from here

and never look back.

Run.

Run.

Run.

Even if it means beginning again.

Every single day, I tell myself

just to get in my car and

hold onto the steering wheel until the car runs out of

gas.

But I'm in too deep to bail.

If I disappear, they'll come looking for me.

They'll make death look easy.

Words pour out of me as potent as my fear, spilling across the paper and splattering ink. With each stroke of the pen, I feel lighter. Freer. But then my "business" phone vibrates from inside my bag. Just like that, the lightness and freedom vanishes from my grasp.

I dig through my bag until I find the phone then swipe my finger across the screen and open up the text message.

Doc: Mcet me in the back parking lot of the bar tonight at nine o'clock. We need to talk about something important. Don't be late. And remember I hate being let down, so whatever I ask you tonight, it's important that you answer correctly.

I swallow the massive lump wedged in my throat as my hands begin to shake. Something's wrong. I can feel it in my bones. Whether it has to do with me sneaking out Emery or with what Brooks said, I'm not sure.

The only thing I'm positive about is that I'll never feel completely free again until this is all over.

Ryler

By the time I arrive back at my apartment, the sun is descending behind the mountains and the sky is various shades of pink and orange. I linger on the stairway, smoking a cigarette and pretending to stare at the sky as the moon rises. Really, I'm trying to get a feel of my surroundings. If any cars look out of place. If any people look out of character. If anyone's attention remains on me for too long.

From what I can tell, nothing appears out of the ordinary, so I head inside, lock myself in my room, and text Stale from my "personal" phone.

Me: I think they might know about Brooks.

Stale: Ryler, we've been through this before. You're always worried they might know, but everything's always been fine.

I flop down on my mattress and rake my fingers through my hair, stressed out beyond imagine.

Me: Brooks was acting strange today. He said someone is watching him. And the other day Doc seemed to know I took Emery out even though we didn't tell anyone.

Stale: Brooks informed me of the same thing, but everything's fine. In fact, I received a text from him earlier.

Fine. Fine. Fine. A fucking placating word he uses all the time.

Me: What did the text say?

Stale: That he thinks he has a lead to where the warehouse is. He's looking into it tonight. This could be big, Ryler.

Strange…

Me: When did he say this to you? Because earlier he was saying he thought the warehouse might not exist.

Stale: He texted me just a couple of hours ago. Don't worry about Brooks. We're perfectly clear on what's going on with him. Everything he's been doing and saying to you has been calculated.

I shake my head. I'm being left out of the loop again. I could press for more details, but knowing Stale, he's not going to tell me anything.

Me: I have to meet Doc tonight. I don't want to, but if you think I should, could you at least send someone to follow me and keep an eye on things?

Stale: I can send Loroney. He's good. He'll keep an eye on things.

Me: Thanks.

Stale: And Ryler, what do you mean you took Emery out the other night? Why didn't you tell me this before?

Me: Because it wasn't a big deal. We just went to a concert. We were bored.

Stale: I think it's good you're taking her out. Just be a little more careful that Doc doesn't find out.

Stale is always pushing for me to try to wiggle details out of Emery. He wants me to find out if she knows the location of the warehouse or if she knows any information about Donny Elderman that might be useful. I feel like an asshole for even thinking of using her like that, though, and avoid making any sort of agreement to do so.

Me: I didn't let him find out that we went out. I'm pretty sure he has someone watching me and they reported it back to him.

I sit up and pull back the curtain. The view is of a park where a ton of people are running around, lying around, and having fun. What if one of Elderman's men is down there, watching my bedroom window? What if they can see me looking out the window?

I release the curtain and lie down, fear pulsating through my veins.

Stale: Even if he does, you've done nothing wrong. All you need to do is make sure it stays that way.

Easy for him to say. He isn't the one in the middle of a world where people get killed for saying the wrong thing. I could only imagine what they'd do to me if they found out I was working for the police.

I text Stale that I will and then hide the phone in my boot.

I'm irked as hell that I even have to go meet Doc. I lie in bed for another hour, drowning my thoughts in music and fighting the urge to punch the wall until it's time to go. I take my gun with me, something I don't normally do, but it seems important tonight.

A half hour later, I'm pulling up behind the bar, a small building located at the end of town near a few stores and gas stations. I park my car beneath the bright stars and moon and silence the engine. Then all that's left to do is wait for whatever comes next.

The gun in my hand leaves my arm feeling detached from my body. If this situation turns deadly, I'm not sure I'll be able to pull the trigger. I'm not a killer, something I've quickly learned over the last few weeks.

Time moves at a snail's pace. Nine o'clock comes and passes. The longer I wait, the more my fear amplifies. I swear I can actually smell death in the air. I should have never showed up. What the hell was I thinking? For all I know, Stale didn't even send his guy to keep an eye on things. Wouldn't be the first time. And what does it even matter if one of his men is here? Once Doc climbs in the car with me, it'll only take a second for him to end my life.

I slump back in the seat, let my head flop back, and stare up at the ceiling. Another twenty minutes tick before I lift my head back up and scan the almost vacant parking lot. Is a cop hiding in one of the cars? Or is it the same people watching Brooks?

A knock on the window sends me jumping in my seat. I whip the gun in the direction of the passenger side as the door opens.

Doc sticks his head into the car, his brows dipping at the sight of the gun in my hand. "Relax," he says, sliding into the passenger seat. "It's just me."

Like that makes me feel better.

My palms sweat as I lower the gun and set it on my lap. "Sorry… I've just been a little paranoid lately with all the shit going on."

By shit, I mean the stuff Doc has been dragging me into. Drug deals gone awry, lives taken, robbery and assault. Over the course of a few weeks, I've seen more blood spilled than anyone should ever have to see.

Doc shuts the car door. "Being paranoid is understandable. I know I've been putting you through a lot lately, but you've been handling it well. Way better than a lot of the trainees."

"I'm trying to be less edgy," I sign, then reach for the cigarettes in my pocket. "I really am, but it's hard."

"I know it is, but I believe you're going to make me proud one day. You're always on time and do whatever you're told. My hopes for you are high."

I attempt to get a read on his vibe. He seems at ease, unlike someone who's about to kill, which should calm me down. But Doc is a relaxed killer.

Doc removes his fedora and rubs his hand over the top of his head. "If only my son could have been like you. His life would have been so much easier for him." With his finger, he draws a cross over his chest and utters something under his breath.

Silence fills the cab. I light the cigarette up and take a long drag, attempting to settle my nerves. I find it odd that Doc speaks of his son in the past tense. He once told me that his son was a drug addict, and I watched Doc kill a drug dealer for selling his son the drugs that ultimately put his son in a coma. His son's still alive, though, not dead.

"Is everything all right?" I sign with the cigarette dangling between my lips.

"As fine as it always is." His voice is sharp, but then he sighs and places the hat on his head. "Sorry, I'm just a little irritated. I've had a rough night." He pauses, his gaze gliding to mine. "I just found out earlier today that one of our own has been working for the police."

A ripple of panic rushes through me and my fingers itch for the gun, but Doc is watching my every move. Every single thing I do and say is going to weigh heavily on the outcome of the situation. One false move on my part, and I could end up dead.

"You know, there's nothing in this world I hate more than a traitor," he mumbles, removing his gun from the holster. "In my opinion, they're the scum of the earth. Going against family like that…. Outing secrets that aren't theirs to share. Family is blood, Ryler. And you never go against blood." He smoothes his hand over the metal, and the silver catches sharply in the moonlight. "If I had my way, I'd off every single traitor."

A chill slithers up my spine. "Who is the traitor?" My heart slams against my chest as I wait for his answer.

His stare is nearly unbearable. "Brooks Dellefondie."

Shit. Brooks said he was being watched. Doc knows I speak to Brooks. What if he knows I'm an informant, too? If he does, then I'm dead where I sit. I'll never see the light of day again.

Just like Brooks.

The thought strikes me like a fist to the stomach, and it takes all my effort not to shove the door open and hurl.

"Brooks? Really?" I gape at him, hoping I look shocked and that I'm not noticeably trembling.

"It was a real shock to me, too, especially for Doug Dellefondie who swears up and down he didn't know about his son's betrayal. It doesn't really matter either way. It's never a good thing to piss Donny off, and he's fucking furious right now." His eyes remain trained on me.

I flick my cigarette out the window. "What's going to happen to them?"

"Brooks will be punished accordingly and so will his father. Doesn't quite seem fair, though, that Doug has to pay for his son's wrongdoings. Sometimes a father can try and try and try and yet their child still turns out to be a bad seed." A faraway look crosses his expression, and I wonder if he's thinking about his son. Or maybe even Emery.

I absentmindedly brush my finger across the scar on my throat, remembering one of the final times my foster father punished me—a branding iron to the throat that seared my voice into oblivion. What kind of punishment will Brooks have to endure? Will it be worse?

"But that's not for you to worry about. I just wanted to tell you in person before the rumors started in our circle. Every time something like this happens, my men seem to turn into gossiping women." Doc reaches across the console and gives me an awkward pat on the shoulder. "You're a good kid, Ryler. I'm proud to have you working with me." He withdraws to put his gun in the holster.

Doc doesn't appear to know I've been working with Brooks, but I can't shake the terrifying thought out of my head that Brooks could be dead, and I could be next.

Fuck! I hope Brooks had time to run, but would it even do any good if he did? Elderman's a powerful man with a lot of connections. Tracking down someone is extremely easy for him.

"The other reason I called you here tonight is that I'd like for you to do me a favor." Doc reaches for the door handle. "Keep an extra eye on Emery over the weekend. Don't let her out of your sight, and by no means are you in any way to take her out."

A slow breath eases from my mouth. "I'm really sorry about that. I messed up big time."

"Yes, you did, but I know it wasn't your fault. I know for a fact my daughter asked you to take her out." When I start to shake my head, he raises his hand in front of him.

"Ryler, watch what you say. I always, *always* know what's going on in my daughter's life. No more arguing. It's clear you're not remembering that night clearly."

I rack my brain for what happened the night Emery and I decided to go out, and a thought occurs to me. Before I decided to take Emery out that night, she'd asked to get out of the house. In reality, it was my fault we left, but she suggested it first. But how in the hell could Doc know that? The only two people who heard her say it were me and Emery herself.

"I need you to do one more thing for me," Doc says, opening the door. "I need you to convince Emery to come back home. She's not doing well out on her own, but she's too stubborn to see that."

"I don't think she'll listen to me." Plus, I talked to Emery enough before all shit hit the fan to understand she's not fond of the home she grew up in.

"Make her listen to you," he presses. "Convince her that her life is at risk. Not only is she ruining the life her mother and I built for her, but the people who left her that note today are a real threat."

"That note today? Did she get a new one?"

He nods, glancing at his watch. "Just after school. In fact, she should be calling to tell me at any moment." He climbs out of the car but then ducks his head back into the cab. "Make her listen to you, Ryler."

"I'll try."

What I really want to know, though, is how in the hell he knows Emery received a note when she hasn't told him.

I think of the last thing Brooks said to me. *They're watching me.*

"Change her mind, Ryler. Convince her to come home," Doc urges. "No matter what lie it takes. Tell her she'll get killed if she doesn't."

"But isn't her life in danger already? I mean, whoever is sending her those notes wants her dead, right?" At least, that's what he's been telling me.

He angles his head to the side, muses over something, and then starts to shut the door. "The only person that's a danger to Emery is Emery herself."

I lean over the console and sign, "What does that mean?"

Without answering, he shuts the door then crosses the parking lot toward the dimly lit bar, whistling a Johnny Cash song. Only when he vanishes out of my sight does the oxygen fully return to my lungs.

What did he mean Emery puts herself in danger? Is he simply referring to the fact that she won't return home? Or is there something more to it than that?

I'm kind of crazy. Did you know that? Did my father tell you? Emery said those words to me at the concert. I hadn't thought too much about it at the time, chalked it up to her being drunk, but I'm starting to wonder if maybe her parents think she's crazy and have somehow convinced her that she is.

I shake the thought from my head. *I'm getting off track.*

Even though it takes a lot of effort, I grab my "personal" phone from inside my boot and send Stale a text.

Me: Brooks is in trouble. They found out about him.

I strangle the shit out of the steering wheel while my heart rate settles. When Stale doesn't text back, I slide the phone back into my boot and focus on driving toward home. It's late enough that most of the stores are closed and the streets are fairly desolate. It gives me the sense that I'm alone in the city, and I let the ease of the feeling sink in, wishing I could grasp onto it.

By the time I park the car at my apartment complex, Stale has had enough time to respond to my text. I fetch it out of my boot, and the inner peace I felt while driving dissipates.

Stale: Don't worry about him. We got him out in time, but we had to pull him out before he could get an exact location on the warehouse.

Me: Where is he?

Stale: I can't tell you that. It's confidential.

I'm not positive I entirely believe him. Stale knows that I spook easily, so I think he keeps a lot of stuff from me because of that. If Brooks has been caught by Donny Elderman, Stale might be worried I'll bail if I find out.

Me: U know they'll find him even if he runs.

**Stale: That's not for you to worry about. You just
need to focus on the warehouse. Have you gotten anywhere with Emery?**

Through the windshield, I peer up to the third floor of
the apartment at Emery's bedroom window. I should just
break down and tell her what's really going on. Emery dis-
likes her father, so maybe she'd help me bring him and the
man he works for down. But what if she didn't? Even
though I know her, I don't know her, *know* her. Not enough
to trust her with my life, anyway.

**Me: I'm still working on her. In fact, I'm going to
work on her now. Talk to you later.**

**Stale: Ryler, we're running out of time. Things are
getting dangerous. I know you're a good guy, but it's
time to make a choice. Emery's got to be the key to getting the location of the warehouse. I know she has to
have an idea of where that warehouse is—I can feel it in
my bones. Get her to trust you and open up to you.
Make this happen. We no longer have Brooks anymore
so this is all on you.**

I blow out a stressed breath as I reread through his words. Using Emery strikes me deep inside my soul. The girl is already broken enough, especially after she thinks I betrayed her and told her father. Now I'm just supposed to what? Crack her even more? I've been fighting against sinking to that low, and I want to continue fighting. But a tiny part of me wants to stop fighting and do whatever I have to do to get out of this double life.

Me: Did you ever maybe consider just asking for Emery's help? She doesn't seem to like her father. She might be willing to give up the location without us tricking her into it.

Stale: Emery could easily be as dangerous as anyone else in Donny's circle. You can't trust her like that.

He's right—I know that—but a voice fills the back of my head. *The night of the concert it felt like I could trust her. That night felt… real. She felt… real. It felt like she opened up to me.*

Me: Fine. I'll keep you updated.

I shove the phone into my boot and climb out of the car. Instead of going straight up to Emery's place, I make a quick stop at my place.

"You look tired," Luke notes the moment I enter the apartment.

He's lounging on the couch with an untouched bowl of popcorn on the coffee table and "Chloroform Perfume" by From Autumn to Ashes is playing from the stereo. Violet is tangled up in his arms, both their clothes are ruffled, and their hair is sticking up in all kinds of directions.

"Sorry," I sign an apology. Clearly, I just interrupted a moment between the two of them.

"No worries," Luke replies as Violet sits up and readjusts her shirt.

She combs her fingers through her red and black hair. "We were just…" She looks to Luke who shrugs.

"We were getting ready to fuck," he tells me.

Violet swats his arm, laughing.

"TMI," I sign to Luke, tearing myself away from my thoughts. I cross the living room, heading for my bedroom. "I'll be out of your hair in a minute."

"You're fine," Violet assures me as she settles onto the couch. "We should be in the bedroom, anyway."

"I still have to leave soon," I sign as I walk backwards. "I'm headed up to Emery's, anyway."

"Everything okay?" Luke calls out before I step down the hallway. "You look upset."

I give him an A-Okay sign without turning around then slip into my bedroom. I immediately shed my clothes and put on a pair of clean jeans and a shirt. Lately, I've felt so disgusting whenever I come back from my night job. I've been changing and taking showers in an attempt to cleanse myself. It never works, though, and I always feel dirty and wrong. I doubt I'll ever feel clean again until I get out of this world and get a fresh start. I just hope I live long enough to do so.

Chapter 9

Mad, Mad World

Emery

My mother used to whisper of drinking the poison.

She never stated what the poison was,

only that she craved the taste of it on her tongue.

Poison that burns the veins, she'd say.

Poison that corrupts the soul.

Poison.

Veins.

Corrupt.

Soul.

117

*I often wonder just how corrupted her scorching soul
and veins are.*

Enough to drive her crazy.

*Just the right dose, and she'll go
mad.*

But that's okay.

This world is already filled with madness, anyway.

*My brother, Ellis, while I loved him, was part of this
madness, too.*

He'd drink the poison like it was water,

clear liquid he needed to purify his blood.

This is what he truly believed.

That poison would save him from the madness,

the darkness of the world.

But I'm starting to wonder if it didn't.

Starting to wonder if maybe it darkened him more.

If he became like my mother,

filled with venom that tainted his blood.

That like my mother, he's rotting inside.

Rotting away.

Never to be saved.

Never to be seen again.

Ellis,

where are you?

I feel like the answer is buried

deep in the unbalance part of my mind.

Once forgotten, but now surfacing

as the poison leaves my mind.

I feel like I see you because I know the truth.

Feel like maybe you're the truth trying to get set free.

But how do I find the truth,

when it's hidden inside me?

"Emery."

My head whips up from my notebook, and I drop my pen on the bed. I relax when I see it's just Ellis hovering in the doorway. Well, relax as much as I can when I'm staring at what could possibly be a hallucination.

"Why are you here this time?" I sit up on the bed, swing my legs over the edge, and plant my feet onto the carpet. "Mother's not coming, is she?"

He shakes his head. "Can't I just drop by to check up on you?" he asks, leaning against the doorframe with his arms crossed.

"You've never done that before," I remind him, sliding the notebook out of the way. "Usually, you come with a warning hidden in a riddle. Or to tell me to beware of Mother and Father, which I already knew. I've known since

I was four and they strapped me to the bed for the first time, all because I dared open the front door at night."

"That was the same night Father took me into the basement and punished me for the first time."

"In the basement? I thought that was where he took the people who betrayed Elderman."

"He did that, too. But sometimes he would take me down there when I betrayed him." He pauses. "Didn't you recognize my screams?"

"Sometimes," I shamefully admit with my head hung low. "But it didn't always sound like you."

"Sometimes I was gagged, but it was usually in the basement… In the basement." His voice echoes at the end.

Bile burns at the back of my throat as the image of our basement flashes through my mind, particularly the blood staining the concrete. "Ellis, I'm so sorry that that happened to you. I should have tried to help you."

"Don't worry about it. What's done is done." He waves me off. "You can't change the past, Emery, but what you can do is change your future."

"And now it's riddle time, right? Could you by chance tell me a riddle I could solve this time? Like why I see you here, yet every time I call back home to talk to you, Mother won't let me speak to you. Or why she gets so angry whenever I mention you. I know she's upset with you, but… it's still so odd."

"Mother never let us speak to each other before you left. You know that. And that's not why I came tonight. I just wanted to see if you're okay." He scans me over, as if checking for visible wounds. He won't see them no matter how hard he looks. Most of my scars are internal, except for the one on my back inflicted by my father. "I had a bad feeling something was about to happen to you."

"If you're not real, how is it possible for you to have a bad feeling?" I wonder, nervously wringing my hands on my lap. "For a hallucination, you seem to know a lot. Maybe it's me that knows stuff… Are you my subconscious trying to tell me stuff I already know?"

"How do you know that I'm not real?" he questions with speculation.

"I have no idea." I rub my eyes exhaustedly. "It seems like you shouldn't be, though. You're basically a ghost."

"You look tired," he observes, changing the subject. "Have you been having trouble sleeping?"

"Sort of. I never seem to be able to fall asleep until almost morning, and by then the day has already begun again." I glance out the window with a sigh.

It's past ten o'clock at night, and the sky is a sheet of darkness splashed with glimmering stars. I'm in my pajamas; boxer shorts and a tank top. My long, brown hair is piled on top of my head, and my face is makeup free. I could blame my appearance on it being late, but it's really because I've had zero energy to do anything since Evan left my place. Not only did he break me down and strip me of every ounce of energy, but the note has been weighing heavily on my mind. So far, I've received three.

Thou shall break.

We're watching you, Emery. You've been a bad, bad girl, and now you're going to pay.

We know what you did.

I haven't told my father about the last one, and I'm unsure if I'm going to since I'm still not positive he isn't the one sending me them. Although the handwriting doesn't always resemble his; he could easily be hiring one of his minions to write them.

"You should tell him," Ellis says abruptly.

"Tell who what?" I ask, redirecting my attention to him.

"You should tell the guy who's always over—the one who can't speak—about the letter on the doorstep."

I swallow a lump in my throat. "Ryler?"

I press my hand to my aching chest. It hurts to think about Ryler, a maddening pain, an invisible wound rubbed with salt. The words he wrote about me fit my life so much. I desperately want him to show up and fix my wilting life. He never did, though, and it isn't his job to do so, anyway. His job is to obey my father.

I want to cry just thinking about it. Cry. Cry. Cry. All the time. Cry because now I'm stuck with Evan who kisses and touches me. Bruises and breaks me. He even broke my bracelet today. Out of fear of my mother finding out again, I secured it to my wrist with a twist tie, but I have no idea what's going to happen to me when she finds out. Part of me terrifyingly doesn't care. With each day, I'm becoming more careless, and I have a feeling that it'll eventually be the death of me.

"I have to tell you something." Ellis straightens from the doorway, crosses the room, and stops a few steps away from me.

"Will it be something I can understand?" I tip my chin back to look up at him. "Or a puzzle for me to solve?"

He smiles, but his expression carries a trace of pain. "I don't have to speak in riddles anymore. You can understand me better now."

"Why? What's changed? Is it because I'm no longer taking the medication? Did it all finally leave my system and all the crazy is allowing me to fully communicate with you?"

He sighs and sits down on the foot of the bed, leaving a mattress length between us. "Your medication is part of the reason things are getting clearer—your mind is getting clear. And because of that—because you're starting to remember—I'm finally finding peace in my life."

He looks utterly miserable. I want to reach out and hug him. I'm afraid to do so, though. Afraid my arms will slip right through him. "I don't understand what you mean."

"I'm saying," he sucks in a gradual breath, "that I found my peace in life because soon I won't be suffering. I almost feel," his eyes drift to the ceiling, "free."

Free. Unlike you are now.

Images surface, thick and heavy like dirt.

Ellis can't breathe.

"How can I help you?" I ask, scooting closer to him. "Tell me what to do."

"All you can do is remember what is and what will never be." When his gaze meets mine again, he shifts his weight and extends a hand toward me, but then he notices the ghostliness of his fingers and draws back. "And now I'm going to say goodbye and warn you to get out of Laramie and go someplace safe. Someplace you can really hide and never be hurt again."

My eyes flick to the fresh bruises on my arms then to the open door of the bedroom. "Is someone coming to get me? The person who left the envelope on my doorstep?"

"Yes, they are. And very soon." He sighs, his silhouette flickering. "I'm so sorry I couldn't save you from what's coming. I'm just hoping you'll finally get peace in your life, too. That you'll let go of the things you couldn't control and stop blaming yourself. Let go, Emery. Please, let me go. Don't continue to torture yourself with things you have no control over."

"Wait… Ellis… What's coming for me? Who left the note?" I leap for him, reaching out as he starts to fade away. "Ellis, please don't go. Not until you tell me what's going on."

"I have to," he tells me with remorse, flickering in and out of focus. "Please, don't turn out like me, Emery. Let the truth set you free."

"Truth?" I gape at him incredulously. "You want me to tell Father the truth?"

"No, only someone you can trust. Truth can only be uttered through trust. Truth and trust are linked."

"I don't know who you mean. Who can I trust?"

"Goodbye," he mouths, and then he's gone.

I'm left staring at the empty bed, wondering if he was ever really there to begin with. He said he was at peace now, maybe even free. But what does that even mean? Where is he? Who is coming after me? Better yet, who can I trust?

You remember that night? The one when you snuck out. What you saw. What you didn't want to see. Think of your father. Think, Emery, think. Think about what happened to Ellis. My thoughts attempt to whisper secrets to me, but I'm not sure about anything anymore, other than this is a mad, mad, mad world I'm living in, and I might be the main thing feeding the madness.

I spend the next ten minutes staring into nothingness until I hear a knock on the front door that triggers a nerve. Ellis warned me someone would be coming. Have they made it here already?

The hairs on the back of my neck stand on end, a spark of static kissing each one as I reach for the metal box hidden beneath my bed. I lift the lid and grab the gun. *For if anyone finds out what you really are, Emery*, my father said when he gave the box to me. I'm not sure what he meant, but... A memory creeps into my mind, one I'd forgotten on purpose.

I want to be at peace.

You'll never be at peace.

"It's better not to exist than to exist in darkness," my father said as he gave Ellis a gun. "Make the choice. Make me proud, son. Don't let your family suffer for your sins anymore."

Ellis chose to drop the weapon to the floor. "I can't do it."

My father, angry and embarrassed, sent Ellis away that night. It was the last time I ever saw him.

I blink from the memory that has been buried in the darkness of my mind, finally spilling out right along with the madness.

The metal of the gun is cold against my clammy hands.

So cold.

So cold like me.

I'm so cold all the time inside.

Carrying the weapon makes me feel sick to my stomach.

Make a choice.

Make a choice.

Make a choice.

I raise the gun as I tiptoe down the hallway. I hear the click of the door unlock and freeze. The door creaks open, and then I hear footsteps.

I should run.

But where would I go?

Make a choice.

Make a choice.

Make a choice.

I click off the safety of the gun and suck in a breath as I point the barrel at the end of the hallway. The person rounds the corner and appears in my line of vision.

Make a choice.

Make a choice.

Make a choice.

My brother chose to put the gun down and paid the consequences. My finger rests on the trigger.

Make.

A.

Choice.

When Ryler sees me, his eyes widen and his hands elevate in surrender. I remain still for a few moments longer, before lowering the gun.

You failed.

A knot winds in my stomach.

When Ryler decides I'm not a threat, his hands fall to his sides. "Why do you have that? " His hands move in front of him as he signs to me.

"Because I heard someone coming in, and I was scared."

"Scared of what?" he signs with curiosity written in his expression.

I shrug. "Go down the list. My father has a ton of enemies. You should know that."

"I do know that." He glances between my face and the gun. Then he cautiously inches forward and reaches for the weapon, carefully watching me as he removes it from my hand.

A breath eases from Ryler's lips once he has the gun. He checks the clip to see how many bullets are in it then shakes his head as he tucks it into the back of his jeans.

"Before you go using a gun, you might want to check to make sure it's loaded," he signs, freeing a trapped breath, seeming relieved.

I press my lips together, feeling idiotic. "I don't know how to load it."

"That's a good thing," he assures me. "You shouldn't be carrying it around. Fuck, you shouldn't even have it in your apartment to begin with. Where did you even get it?"

"My father gave it to me," I say flatly. "Where else would I have gotten it?"

He hesitates then raises his hands in front of him to sign, "Well, I'm going to hang onto it."

"But I need it for…" What am I supposed to say? I have hallucinations of my brother, and he warned me someone is coming for me. That there was a bloody note on the doorstep, left by someone who knows my dirty, little secret and wants to kill me.

I stupidly told Ryler during the night of the concert that I'm crazy. I never fully explained why, and I'm sure he probably chalked it up to me being drunk. If I told him about my brother, though, he might run for his damn life.

But isn't that what I want,

for him to go,

because I don't trust him?

Right?

Right?

Right?

I honestly don't know.

"Why are you looking at me like that?" Ryler wonders with his brows knit. "What's wrong?"

"It's nothing." I force a yawn and stretch my arms above my head. "I'm just tired. I should really get to bed."

"You want me to make you some coffee?" he offers. "Or we could go get some. I know it's late, but there's a café a couple of blocks away that stays open late."

"No, I don't want you to break the rules again and take me out. The last thing I need is another visit from my mother." I wait for him to take the hint and leave, even though only part of me wants him to go.

He studies me with his head slanted to the side. "I can't go," he signs. When I frown, he adds, "Sorry, but your father told me to stay with you tonight."

My gaze wanders over my shoulder to my bedroom, specifically the bed. My skin tingles at the idea of being in that bed with him again. It felt so wonderful to sleep in his arms, to be held like that, and oddly, at the time, I'd felt safe. If he stayed again, he could erase all the memories of what Evan did to me. But what happens when morning rolls around? Would he go to my father and report everything we did?

"What's going on? Why is he making you stay the night with me?" When I look at Ryler again, I find him staring at my chest. I tip my chin down then internally cringe at the sight of my nipples poking through my shirt.

My body betrays me as it hums to life from his attention. I cross my arms over my chest, and Ryler tears his gaze away and awkwardly scratches the back of his neck.

"Something's been going on with his business. He's pissed off some people or something, I'm guessing." He pauses, chewing nervously on his bottom lip. "How much do you know about what your father does?"

"How much do *you* know about what he does?" I quip with my brows elevated in insinuation.

We exchange an intense look, and life sparkles inside me. But then I wonder how many secrets Ryler keeps from me, and the life fizzles and dies. Still, I end up caving first, his gaze too overwhelming for me to endure.

When I look away, he hooks a finger under my chin and forces my attention back to him. My heart jolts in my chest from his touch as the skin-to-skin contact lavishly warms my body.

Then he pulls his hand away, leaving me chilly again. "You don't need to be afraid of me, Emery," he signs. "I'm not the enemy here. I don't want to hurt you, only help you."

Truth and trust go together hand in hand.

But I don't trust anyone.

Not even Ryler.

I might have once.

But now that trust has evaporated to dust.

"You work for my father." My tone is off-pitch, uneven, laced with fear from everything I felt today when I found the envelope and when Evan forced me down on my bed. "Therefore, you *are* the enemy in my eyes. You proved that when you told him about the concert."

Uttering something negative about my father to anyone who knows him has me terrified out of my damn mind. But Ryler needs to understand that we're not friends, even if he did write beautiful poetry about me and took me out for one of the best nights of my life. Even if his touch makes me feel… something.

Two seconds later, reality crashes down on me, though. I realize what I've done, how big of a mistake I just made.

"Oh, God, please don't tell him that." I shuffle away from Ryler. "Please, please, please don't tell him." I back down the hallway like a skittish cat. Tears well up in my eyes and regret seeps into my bones. "I didn't mean it," I whisper. "My father's not a bad person. He just cares about me."

Ryler steps toward me, but I quicken my pace, putting more distance between us.

He freezes, his eyes swirling with confusion as he lifts his hands and signs, "What are you so afraid of? Please, just tell me." He seems torn. "I can help you... If someone is trying to hurt you, I can help you."

What am I afraid of?

God, there are so many things.

My father.

My mother.

Evan.

Where Ellis could possibly be.

My mind.

My sanity.

My lips part, ready to feed him a lie, but the truth slips out, the thing that scares me the most.

"I'm afraid of never getting out of this life unless it's in a coffin."

Chapter 10

Drowning in Emotion

Ryler

"I'm afraid of never getting out of this life, unless it's in a coffin," Emery whispers, her eyes glassy as tears spill down her cheeks.

She's terrified out of her damn mind, even more so than she normally is. Afraid. Of her father. Of her mother. Of Evan. Of me. The list probably goes on and on. I fucking hate that I'm on that list. If I could, I'd take her in my arms and tell her the truth.

After about thirty seconds of panicking, Emery rushes off to her room and slams the door. I contemplate knocking, then decide to give her space and head for the living room to wait it out. I clean up some candy wrappers and empty soda cans from off the table, then flop down on the sofa.

My phone buzzes the moment my ass sinks into the cushion. Sighing, I fish out my "business" phone, loathing answering it just as much as my "personal" one.

Doc: I need u to do me another favor tonight. It's extremely important.

Me: I thought I was supposed to watch Emery tonight?

Doc: Take her with you so you can keep an eye on her. I don't want her alone anymore for a while. Plus, she can translate for you.

Me: Okay.

Doc: Go to the west side of the city near Desingfield Blvd. Do you know where that is?

Me: I do. You want me to leave right now?

Doc: No, this is going to be an early morning call. Be there by four. I won't be at the place, but Moleney knows you're coming. It's his house. He'll give you the package.

My lip twitches. Evan Moleney. Emery's ex-boyfriend who's the biggest douche I've ever met. I hate that he's the one who picks her up from school. That he's the one who gets to touch her and kiss her like I did during those brief moments when Emery and I didn't know who the other was.

Me: What am I supposed to do with it when I get the package? Drop it off at the bar?

Doc: No. Hang on to it for me. I'll be there tomorrow to pick it up.

Me: Okay, I'll get Emery and head out in a little bit.

Doc: Take your gun with you.

My muscles wind tight as my gut instincts scream not to go. Beg me to walk away from this. Maybe it's time. I'll just take Emery and run. Would she come with me if I did?

Instead, I text back.

Me: Okay.

I shove the phone into the pocket of my faded black jeans. I hate guns. Hate that Doc gave me one of my own. Hated seeing Emery with one in her hand.

I drag my ass off the sofa and walk down the hallway toward Emery's room. On my way, I pass this wall piece; a wooden circle with angled shapes and circular patterns. The damn thing gives me the creeps and not just because I've seen the symbol on a lot of Elderman's men. There's something about it, something I can't quite put my finger on, that makes me want to light the thing on fire and watch it burn.

I'm not sure what the meaning of the symbol is, but I know it's Donny's brand. A few guys have tried to convince me to tattoo the symbol on my body. I have to be cautious to never agree, yet never outright refuse, otherwise, I'll come off as suspicious.

I tap my knuckles on her bedroom door. When I hear a muffled cry from the other side, I squeeze my eyes shut. I haven't known Emery for that long, but during the brief time we've spend together, I've developed strong feelings for her. Whenever she's sad, scared, or in pain, it nearly breaks my fucking heart.

Wrapping my fingers around the doorknob, I push the door open. The lights are off, but a trail of moonlight flows through the window and onto the bed. Emery is curled in a ball, facing the wall, with her arms wrapped around herself.

"I don't want to talk anymore," she murmurs. "Just, please, leave me alone." Her shoulders begin to shake as she soundlessly cries.

I yank my fingers through my hair, trying not to lose control over who I'm supposed to be at the moment. Ryler who works for Doc—the Ryler who cares about his job more than anything else. Still, it's hard to remain in control when I'm witnessing the most beautiful girl with the saddest eyes fall apart right in front of me.

Without too much forethought, I slide onto the bed with her. The mattress caves beneath my weight as I scoot closer. Her breath hitches in her throat, and her body goes as rigid as a board the second my chest brushes her back.

I hesitate before reaching toward her back and tracing on the fabric of her shirt, *Not going to hurt you.* I place my hand on her arm.

She flinches from my touch, but doesn't pull away. Her skin is incredibly warm… God, I've forgotten how warm and inviting she is.

Sucking in an uneven breath, I give her shoulder a soft tug. When she rotates toward me, I sit up and sign, "Tell me what's wrong."

"I can't tell you," she replies, her face hidden in the shadows.

"Why not?"

A second or two trickles by before she moves out of the shadows and into the moonlight. I can see her perfect, full lips I've tasted a few times. Her pale skin is like porcelain, and her big eyes reflect her raw, inner pain.

"You know why I can't." She rotates all the way onto her back and props up on her elbows, putting our lips only inches apart and forcing me into a position to either move back or kiss her.

Even though it's agonizing, I don't choose the latter.

"I don't know why, Emery. I really don't," I sign.

Stale's text flashes through my mind. I tell myself that what I do next is because of what he said, but deep down I know the truth—that the only reason I'm here with Emery is because I want to be.

I graze my finger across her cheek, causing her breath to hitch in her throat. My heart erratically pounds. "But you can always tell me. I know things have been rocky between us since your father assigned me as your bodyguard, but I'm still the same guy I was before. Nothing's really changed. I'm still a good listener, and I still enjoy spending time with you."

"Still the same? No, I don't think so. I wish nothing had changed, but you're part of my father's world, Ryler, despite how much I try to convince myself that isn't true. You telling him we went out… That was a big reminder." She searches my eyes as if the truth of who I am is in there. Part of me wants her to see it, wants her to see who I really am. "No, everything's different." She raises her arm to scratch her forehead, and I spot circular marks on her skin.

"What happened?" I point at the bruises on her wrists.

She swiftly moves to tuck her arm behind her, but I capture her it, my fingers gently folding around her wrist. I lean in so my lips are close. *"Tell me,"* I mouth.

Her chest heaves as she breathes raggedly. She's not wearing a bra, something I noticed when I arrived at her house. Her nipples are visible through her shirt, and the sight is driving me mad, but not as much as the bruises on her skin. Someone hurt her. And recently.

"I can't tell you," she says again, her voice cracking. "I can't tell you anything anymore."

Frustrated, I release her wrist and lean back. "Look, I know I fucked up telling your father, but I didn't have a choice. I promise if there had been a way out of it, I wouldn't have told him." I scoot closer to her and her breathing quickens, her chest heaving. "I want to help you, but you have to tell me what's wrong or else I can't. And I promise that this time your secret will be safe." When her lips remain fused, I search for the right words to get her to open up to me, because I *need* to know who hurt her more than I need anything else at the moment. "Look, I get the whole secret thing. You don't trust me, and it's my fault." I reach over and switch on the lamp before sitting back on the bed.

Emery blinks her bloodshot eyes against the bright light. "I want to, but I just can't anymore." She rests against the headboard, staring at me as she aligns the pads of her fingers with the bruises on her arm. "I don't trust you,

Ryler. And honestly, I don't think you understand how hard it is to keep secrets."

"But I do… I keep secrets every day."

"Keeping my father's secrets isn't the same thing as what I'm talking about. I mean, your own secrets, the kind so potent it nearly kills you every day not to utter the truth."

"I'm not talking about your father's secrets… I'm talking about my own secrets." The gun pokes at my back as I situate against the wall. How far do I want to go with this? How close do I want to get to her? *Really close*, I think, *but not like this*.

Stale's text replays in my mind. *You can't trust her.*

Looking at her right now, with her eyes wide and filled with terror and bruises on her skin, it feels like she's just a victim, not the enemy. Every time I look at her, it feels that way.

What I wrote about her is the truth. She looks as if she's withering away and needs help. I used to feel the same way. All the damn time. Still do.

"I've never told you how I lost my voice." I wait until she fixes her attention on me before I continue. "I grew up in a lot of foster homes when I was younger, and I spent a lot of my life feeling unwanted, betrayed… alone. When I was about sixteen, I ended up with this one guy… Ben. He was a fucking douche bag from hell. He had a few other foster children and was solely in it for the money." I ball my hands into fists as anger, resentment, and pain blaze like fire under my skin. I've never told anyone about this except for Stale and his partner, and the only reason that happened was because they dug up my file.

"There was this girl living there… Aura. She made me feel not so alone. At the time, I thought I loved her." I suck in an unsteady breath. "But now I realize it was more of an infatuation. That I was infatuated with the fact that she seemed to be able to see me." I give a sidelong glance in Emery's direction and discover she's watching me intently, soaking in every single word I sign.

I shift my weight, face her, and look her directly in the eyes. "One day, Ben beat the shit out of her. I stepped in and beat the shit out him back, enough that he ended up in the hospital. I thought I was doing the right thing. Maybe I was. Maybe I wasn't. I'm still not sure. But it doesn't matter. Right or wrong, Ben lied and said I'd started it, said that the reason why he stabbed me in the throat with a fire poker was to protect himself. He said I was the one who beat Aura, said I was violent and had a temper."

Emery glances at the scar on my throat, and her fingers start drifting toward my neck. Then her eyes widen, and she quickly draws back. "Sorry."

"You're fine." I continue on, hoping my story will allow her to see the damage secrets can do instead of her ending up more scared of me. "I'm not going to lie. I wasn't a saint. I had a lot of marks against me. Fights at school. Fights with some of my foster parents. Fights with a few police officers. I had a lot of anger in me for my parents giving me up, and I took it out on a lot of people. Ben was probably the first justifiable fight I'd been in, but the damage had already been done. People only saw me as the fucked up, angry guy I'd been in the past. That's the thing—once you choose to be someone, it's really hard to erase that choice. Is it possible? Sure. But it takes a lot of time." Time that I need. That's all that I want—time to be free and turn into the good person I want to be.

"What about Aura?" Emery finally speaks, her voice as smooth as honey, and her brows are furrowed in confusion. "Didn't she tell the police what really happened?"

I shake my head. "She wouldn't speak up. I'm not sure if it was because she was afraid or what, but it doesn't really matter. She didn't speak up, and I was sent to juvie for two years for assault."

"That's not fair," she says furiously, sitting up straight on the bed. "She should have spoken up. The only reason you got into the fight in the first place was to protect her."

"Not everything in life is fair." I give a half-shrug. "When I think back, I remember how afraid she always was of Ben. I'm guessing that's why she didn't speak up—that he sort of silenced her with fear."

I'm hoping two things will come out of my story. Learning a little bit more about me will hopefully get Emery to trust me more. And maybe she'll realize that doing what's right isn't always the easiest thing. That she may be afraid of her father, but she still needs to speak up about the stuff he does. I want Stale to be wrong about her. Want Emery to be good.

"Fear is pretty toxic, isn't it?" she mutters. "It's hard to see past it."

I nod, my gaze smoldering. "Yes, it is."

She stares at me for a beat longer, and then her gaze zeroes in on my lips. "I'm so sorry that happened to you... Even if you do work for my father," she whispers more to herself. "Adults can be so cruel to the people they take care of, can't they?"

I nod, and then suddenly, her lips crash into mine. The kiss is as rough as the first one we shared, forceful, bruising. My muscles instantly tense from the connection.

Wrong. This has to be wrong. The last thing I should be doing is kissing Doc's daughter, especially when I don't even know the reason why I'm kissing her. Want. Need. Wrong. Right. Where's the line?

Stop it. I need to stop it.

My brain must disconnect from my limbs because, instead of pulling away, I dive dangerously into the kiss. Emery gasps against my mouth and starts to move away, as if sharing the same protesting thoughts. Then she slips her fingers through the hair on the back of my head and kisses me with so much desperation my lip ring sears her lips.

"Oh, God… I've forgotten… how good… this feels," she moans, her voice filled with fear and ecstasy.

The sound of her voice turns me on, hardening my cock in my jeans. Fuck, what I wouldn't give to be inside her. I can't cross that line, though, not when she doesn't know who I truly am.

Every coherent, rational thought drifts from my mind, though, when Emery spreads her legs and grinds against me. A throaty groan escapes my lips as she does the movement again.

Scorching with need, I slide my hand up her side and graze my thumb across the outside of her breast. Her nipple hardens from underneath the fabric, and I damn near lose control. I bite her bottom lip and thrust my hips against hers, eliciting another moan from her. The sound is mind blowing, and the feel of her body heat is like fucking nirvana. I want more. Need more. Need to keep going, need to forget for just two damn seconds all the shit going on.

So, I keep going, falling blindingly into an abyss I'm not sure I can get out of.

Emery and I move rhythmically together, our bodies aligning perfectly.

Perfect.

Perfect.

Perfect.

That's what this moment feels like, even though perfection isn't supposed to exist.

Gasping, our tongues and legs tangle together. My fingers circle one of her wrists, and I start to move her arm above her head, but I pause when she winces.

"Don't stop," she begs, her fingers traveling down my stomach toward the button of my jeans. "Please, Ryler, don't stop."

The ache in her voice makes me go against the rational part of my mind. I start kissing her again with every single ounce of emotion I've kept trapped inside me since I first met her. As the lust, need, longing, aching pours out, I realize just how much I feel for Emery. So much that I'm drowning in it.

Drowning.

Drowning.

Drowning.

So far down in the water I'm not sure I'll ever be able to breathe again.

And I'm not sure I want to.

Chapter 11

Lost My Damn Mind

Emery

I've lost my damn mind, more than I already had. I don't even know why I opened up to Ryler. He was saying all those things about Aura, and he seemed so human, so real. As someone who understands what it is like to have the people you care about hurt you, I momentarily forgot who he works for, saw a different side of him, one I almost feel like I can trust. Like me, Ryler has hurt someone unintentionally.

Like me.

Like me.

Like me.

It feels like Ryler and I are so similar.

God, how I want that to be true.

I've never had sex because I wanted to. God, do I want to have sex with Ryler. So much that I forget about everything and bask in the freedom of knowing nothing.

I only remove my lips to peel Ryler's shirt off, then toss the fabric aside and trace my fingers across his pale flesh inked with poems, lyrics, patterns, and swirls of colors.

"You're so beautiful," I mutter, blushing a little when he chuckles.

"So are you," he mouths, gazing down at me, his fingers lingering near the hem of my shirt. *"You're so pretty."*

My blush deepens as I remember the night of the concert and how I called him pretty. My embarrassment is short lived as he grabs the bottom of my shirt, and I sit up so he can take it off. Then our chests and lips collide, and our tongues tangle as our hands wander all over each other's flesh, feeling and tasting each other completely.

The feel of his metal lip ring grazing my tongue is mind blowing, but then his finger brushes my nipple, and that's when I lose it. A whimper flees my lips, and my back arches into his touch. He groans in response, pinching a little harder.

"Ryler," I whisper breathlessly against his lip as I slip my hand downward toward the top of his jeans again. My fingers fumble to get the button undone then I draw down his zipper.

He momentarily pauses, confliction filling his eyes as he stares down at me. I get where the indecision is stemming from. So many secrets swirl in the air between us, but for once in my life, I want to have what I want at the moment I want it without anyone telling me I can't have it. Perhaps, if I can just do it, do what I want for once without fearing the consequences, I'll finally get the strength to run away and never look back.

"Please," I practically beg, telling myself that the Ryler I want is the one I first met. Nothing more. Nothing less.

With a deep breath, he moves back and flicks the button of my shorts undone, silently agreeing to be with me. The fact that he gives into me makes me believe that somewhere beneath the Ryler who works for my father lays the Ryler I first met—the one who gave me a few fleeting moments away from reality.

My body shivers as he drags the zipper down, his knuckles grazing against my flesh. My breathing quickens into short, erratic breaths, and my nipples harden as my chest heaves.

After he pauses, he gazes down at me. *"Are you sure?"* he mouths.

When I nod, something snaps inside both of us. The calculated movements turn helpless and panicky, as if we're both afraid the moment is going to vanish before our eyes. The rest of our clothes get shed, and then his body covers mine.

We nip at each other's flesh, nails scratching to hold on as our hips grind together. I grip on to his shoulder blades, kissing him deeply, waiting for him to slip inside me. Instead, he continues to kiss me, his fingers traveling across the curve of my breast, along my ribcage, to my hip. He strokes my skin, tracing small circles, before his hand drifts between my legs. With his knees, he urges my legs open, and I easily give in.

When his finger slips inside me, I gasp, biting down on his bottom lip hard. He groans and then kisses me deeply, sucking on my tongue while his fingers move between my legs, driving me toward the edge.

Right as I'm about to fall, though, he removes his fingers and pushes away from me.

Horror seeps into my bones that he doesn't want this as much as me.

Pushing up on my elbows, I reach for my blanket to cover up, but stop when I realize he has only climbed off me to grab a condom from his wallet.

I lie back down and count my breaths, telling myself that what I'm about to do is okay. That I want it and that's enough. That it's okay to want sex.

My thoughts calm as Ryler situates above me. He brushes my hair out of my face and stares deeply into my eyes as he rocks forward, slowly easing into me. I shut my eyes and start to move with him, our hips moving so rhythmically it's like we were made for each other.

As long as I keep my eyes shut, I can almost pretend that's true. That we're two people who care about each oth-

er, who found each other in the darkness. Who are connected.

What I wouldn't give to keep my eyes shut and hold on
to that version of the truth forever. Hold on to this version
of Ryler forever and never, ever let go.

Chapter 12

Buried Alive

Ryler

As I lie awake, staring up at the ceiling of Emery's bedroom, I try to put together what happened over the course of the last two hours. I told Emery about Aura and my past, and then Emery and I had sex. Fuck, it was unbelievable, like our bodies created poetry.

"What are you thinking about?" Emery wonders, propping up on her arm and staring down at me. Her hair is a tangled mess around her face, her eyeliner is smeared, and her skin is sheen with sweat.

"About you and me." I reach for her face and stroke her cheek, wondering what to do next. Where do I go from here? Where do *we* go from here? "How about you?"

She gives a half shrug, her lips quirking to a small smile. "How good that felt."

161

I can't help chuckling and reach to lace our fingers together, but she winces from my touch. I glance down at her arm and realize that she never did tell me who hurt her.

I brush my thumb across one of the bruises on the inside of her wrists. *"Who did this to you?"* I mouth.

She shakes her head again, her expression turning stone cold as she sits up, pressing the sheet to her chest. "Please don't bring that up again. I can't tell you. If I do, I'll be in danger."

I think about the conversation I had with Doc. He said Emery only puts herself in danger. Did she… Did she hurt herself?

"Tell me who did that to you," I sign with a firm expression as I sit up in the bed. "I need to know."

"I already told you, Ryler, I can't tell you." Her eyes silently plead for me to understand as she hugs the sheet to her chest.

Her lips are swollen from my kisses, and her skin is flushed. All I want to do is kiss her again, drown in her instead of my worry. Go back to an hour ago and be inside her again.

But I need to know who hurt her, more than I did before.

My hands speak for me as I kneel down on the bed in front of her. "Please, just tell me. I care about you and need to know who hurt you, otherwise, it's going to drive me crazy."

She nervously chews on her fingernails. "It doesn't matter. None of this does. You can't change what happened to me no matter how much I want you to be able to."

"How do you know that for sure? Maybe I'm not the person you think…" I trail off, wincing at my words.

She carries my gaze, meticulously studying my expression. "You work for my father," she says more to herself.

No, I don't work for your father. Not really. My lips long to utter the truth—long to utter anything—but like always, I bite back the truth. "It's just a job."

"Is it?" she questions with a drop of hope in her eyes. "A lot of my father's acquaintances would disagree with you."

"Well, I'm not them."

"I want to believe that." She rests her chin on her knees, her bottom lip slightly jutted out. "After what just happened between us, I want you to be the guy I first met. The one I keep trying to convince myself exists, but I'm not sure I can."

"Why not?"

"Because you work with the person who hurt me."

"Your dad did that to you?" I gape at her, even though I'm not shocked.

"You look so shocked, yet you know who my father is. How much of a monster he is," she says with her brow curved. "How is that so?"

"I don't know." I'm nervous talking about her father, worried I might let the truth accidentally slip out. My fingers and lungs ache for a cigarette, a dose of nicotine to settle my nerves. "Because you're his daughter... I didn't think he'd hurt you."

A soft, hollow laughs slips from her lips and then she stares at me long and hard. "I think if you really knew him, you'd know that he'll hurt anyone who doesn't abide by his rules, even his own flesh and blood."

I don't know how to respond to what she said. I want to tell her that I'll beat the shit out of Doc for hurting her, but I'd be sentencing myself to death if I tried. But good God, I need to help her somehow.

Her shoulders sag, misinterpreting my silence. "It wasn't my father, anyway. It was Evan, which is worse."

"Evan, your ex-boyfriend? He's the one who hurt you?" When she nods, anger ripples through me like a violent thunderstorm. "When?"

"This morning," she mumbles with a shrug. "After class… He gets rough with me sometimes… All the time actually. Even on our first date, he gripped my wrist so tight I bruised, all because I suggested we go to a movie instead of a party."

The idea of Evan being in her place, touching her, hurting her… forcing her? "Did he… did he force you to do stuff?"

She shrugs again, her eyelashes fluttering as she fights back tears. "He does all the time. Has for years." She sucks back the tears. "Up until recently, I thought that's how things were supposed to be but… How can they be so different with you? I don't get it." She huffs in frustration, pressing her hand to her forehead, stressed out. "I don't get it. I'm not supposed to be this comfortable with someone who works for my father. I'm not supposed to be with someone who isn't part of this world. Someone like the you I first met."

"I am the guy you first met," I assure her, trying to remain calm. I want to ram my fist into Evan's face, watch blood spill from his nose, do the same to him as I did to Ben. "I want to beat the shit out of Evan."

"You don't have to do anything to him. That's not why I told you—so you could go risking your life." She lowers her hand to her lap. "I get it. Evan is Evan. Everyone hates him but has to respect him because he's Donny's son." She rolls her eyes and shakes her head.

My jaw drops. Evan is Donny Elderman's son? What the fuck? How did I not know about this?

Emery reads the shock on my face, and she slaps her hand across her mouth. "Oh, my God. You didn't know who he is, did you?" Tears bubble in her eyes. "I thought you knew Evan is Donny's son. I thought… because you were so close to my father… Oh, my God. Oh, my God.

They're going to kill me. They're going to kill me." She folds her arms around herself and scoots away from me.

I think about all the signs I missed that made Evan's real identity pretty obvious. Evan has bodyguards. He's protected at all times. He's in charge of important tasks, but never actually does the dirty work.

"I'm not going to say anything to anyone," I assure her, dipping my head to meet her teary gaze. "It doesn't even matter who he is. At least not to me." My gut twists at my lie. It does matter. A lot.

This bit of information could be my ticket out of here. Could I do that to Emery? Betray her like that? A few weeks ago, I might have been able to say yes. Now, I'm not sure I can, not when I'm starting to care so much about her.

"Yes, it does matter." Hot tears stream down her cheeks, leaving streaks on her skin. Her eyes are glossy and round, and her hair is tangled around her face. Still, she looks absolutely amazing, so perfect, so untouchable. *Yet, she let me touch her in the most intimate, trusting way possible only an hour ago.* "No one's supposed to know Evan's out here."

"Out here?" My head cocks to the side as pucker forms at my brow. "What do you mean?"

"Out in Laramie instead of…" she trails off, looks toward the wall, and wipes her face with the back of her hand. "I've already said too much. God, I just need to stop talking."

My heart pounds deafeningly from inside my chest. Emery knows where the warehouse is. I can feel it. But how can I get her to speak about it when she's so terrified simply thinking about it?

Fear.

I know how toxic it is.

How it can possess one's soul.

Devour your mind, your body

and swallow you whole.

"Why is Evan here in Laramie, anyway?" I sign cautiously.

"I don't know," she mutters, staring at the floor, avoiding eye contact with me.

Before I get a chance to press her for more information, she straightens her legs and stands to her feet. "I think it might be time for you to leave," she says, seeming torn. "I don't want to talk about this stuff anymore. I shouldn't have told you anything in the first place."

I don't know what to say to her. I know what I want to say, but want and need are entirely different things.

I'm not who you think I am.

I'm as lost as you.

I just want to be free.

You and me, we're not so different.

Night and morning on the outside, we're simply day on the inside.

"I can't leave you alone tonight," I finally sign with an apologetic look. "I have to take you somewhere with me and then stay with you until your father says it's okay for you to be alone."

Her expression plummets. "Where are you taking me?"

"To…" I wince, my hands freezing in mid-air. After what we were just talking about, how can I say it? "To Evan's to pick something up for your father."

Her features harden as she glares at me. I don't know if I've ever seen her so infuriated, so angry.

"Fine," she says through gritted teeth. "Let me get dressed."

She ushers me toward the door with a wave of her hand, and I head to step out, picking up my clothes on the way.

"I'm sorry," I sign as I step out into the hallway.

"For what?" Her voice wobbles.

I fix my gaze on her, hoping she'll see the truth. That I am sorry and that I do care about her. "For everything."

"Me too." She smashes her lips together then closes the door.

The walls rattle and the wooden symbol on the wall slips off one nail, hanging crookedly. I watch it swing back and forth as I get dressed.

Out of all the goddamn people we have to meet to-night, why the fuck does it have to be Evan? Donny fucking Elderman's son. Donny fucking Elderman's son who bruised Emery.

My patience is going to be tested.

I want to bang my head on the door.

Pound a hole into the wall.

Scream until my lungs burst.

But like always, all I can do is remain silent as more secrets push me down into the dirt. I'm starting to believe that I'll never be unburied again. That this life will be my final resting place, and the peaceful moment Emery and I just shared will never be again.

Die.

Die.

Die.

Slowly.

Letting your secrets bury you alive.

Chapter 13

The Truth Will Set You Free, or it Will Kill You

Emery

After telling Ryler about Evan, I'm pretty much a dead woman walking. Ellis warned me someone is coming after me. Maybe that's who is going to end me. Perhaps Ellis saw into the future and knew I was going to mess up, knew my father or Evan would come after me because I couldn't keep my mouth shut. I've always wondered if my father might have been the one behind the notes in an attempt at scaring me to run home.

Regardless of my impending death, I secretly hope that when Ryler and I meet up with Evan, Ryler will lose his shit and punch him for hurting me.

God, I really am insane.

Delusional.

A danger.

More potent than the poison my mother drinks.

My lips are toxic.

My hands are death.

My mind is venomous.

Rain drizzles from the clouds rumbling above us, and silver flashes of lightning light up the cab of the car as we drive down the road toward Evan's. He let me pick the music, and not knowing any bands, I clicked on a random playlist that fills up the silence between us until Ryler turns the volume down while we're stopped at a red light.

"What are you thinking about?" Ryler signs. "You seem upset… Is it because of where we're going?"

I shrug, turning to stare out the window, watching the rain trickle down the glass. It's after three o'clock in the morning and the homes and stores lining the street are pitch black. The lampposts are the only light in the darkness engulfing the sleepy city.

I feel Ryler staring at me until the light turns green. Then he rips his attention off me. Instead of driving forward, he shoves the gearshift into park, leaves the engine idling, and rotates in his seat.

"What are you doing?" I sit up in the seat, glancing around at the desolation around us. "Why aren't you driving?"

"I want you to tell me what's wrong." Ryler's hands circle the air in smooth, flawless movements. "I feel like I should turn around, take you back to my place, and leave you with Violet and Luke. You shouldn't have to see Evan."

"It doesn't matter where I am. Nothing matters," I mumble, looking out the window again as thunder booms. The stores, while masked by darkness, feel alive and awake, as if they're watching me. "And I've already told you too much for the night." I glance back at him again. "You and I have crossed a lot of lines tonight."

"That's arguable," he signs, his eyes burning fiercely. "But we'll talk about that when we get home. Right now, I want you to tell me what's bothering you. And don't tell me that you've told me enough. You haven't told me any-thing really."

I shake my head. "I've told you more than I've told anyone."

"Why are you so untrusting toward everyone?" he wonders. "What's been done to you to make you so scared?"

Truth and trust. He wants me to hand it over, and oh, how I wish I could.

I bite down on my bottom lip until I draw blood, let-ting the foul taste of salt and rust burns at the back of my throat.

"Silence, Emery, or I will cut off your tongue," my mother once said.

Silence, Emery, or I will silence you.

Silence, Emery, silence.

Silence, Emery.

They're going to kill you.

Truth and trust.

Who do you believe?

I want to believe someone.

I want to be set free.

I have nothing left to lose.

My rose petals are all dying and are about to fall to the ground.

It feels like maybe Ryler will pick them up, if I let him.

"My father's going to kill me." My lips move on their own accord, making my decision for me. I keep my head turned away from him, too afraid that I'll see disgust in his eyes. "When he finds out what I've told you—that he's hurt me and so has Evan—they'll both come after me."

Ryler captures my chin in his hand and forces me to look at him. Our gazes drink each other in and then his palm leaves my skin. His hands rise in the air, but then lightning snaps in the sky, and we both jump.

He lets out a shaky breath before he continues. "No one's going to ever find out," he assures me, one side of his mouth lifting into a lopsided grin. "My lips are sealed, and

I mean it this time. What I did… agreeing to..." he trails off, gulping.

"Agree to what?"

He clenches the wheel, taking shallow breaths before elevating his hands again. "Your father told me to tell you I told him we went to the concert that night. I never told him. He just somehow knew." He blows out a freeing breath while I struggle to breathe. "I never should have agreed to lie to you like that."

"But how did he know?" I whisper. "How does he know *everything*?"

Ryler reaches across the console and gives my hand a squeeze before signing, "I don't know how he knows stuff, but I wish I did. I want you to understand that you can trust me." He draws an *X* across his heart. "I'm not Evan. I'm not your father. I'm just Ryler. The guy you first met, the one who gave you back your journal pages without reading them, who taught you how to play poker, who you gave the most amazing kiss ever—that's still me. And what happened tonight was simply amazing. I want more of that if you'll let me."

I suck my bottom lip between my teeth. Blood still lingers on it and the foul taste fills my mouth again. I want it, too, but don't know how it's possible. "My father won't ever let you be with me. I'm supposed to be with Evan. It's been predetermined since I was born."

"We'll figure something out."

He looks like he means it, but again, how?

How can he think us being together, going against my father, is possible?

"Will you tell me why you work for him? My father, I mean. Maybe if you explained it to me, then I'd understand you more. Maybe I could understand why someone who seems as nice as you can work for someone as horrible as him."

His expression drops as he tenses. *"I can't,"* he mouths with remorse.

I look away, fighting back the tears. "It's fine. I understand." But I don't. Not at all.

He grunts in frustration, the sound startling, like every sound he makes. Then his fingers find my chin again, and he urges me to look at him. *"I want to, but I can't,"* he mouths. *"Not right now, anyway."*

"When then?"

"I don't know," his lips move. *"But I'm going to find a way."*

The streetlights reflect across his face, highlighting the pain in his eyes.

I nod, not knowing what else to say.

His fingers leave my face, and he retrieves a pack of cigarettes and a lighter from his pocket. He pops one between his lips then cups his hands around his mouth and lights it up. Smoke immediately snakes through the air, and he cracks the window down. Wind gusts inside along with a spritz of rain.

I expect him to drive. No one's around, but I don't think there's anything left to say to each other except the truth. And neither of us seem willing to cave. Still, Ryler remains motionless, staring out the window, puffing on his cigarette.

Only when he's smoked half of it does he focus back on me again with the cigarette resting between his lips. "What if I told you I didn't want to work for your father?" he asks. "What if I had to work for him, but only for a while?"

I fiddle with the bracelet on my wrist. "Okay… But why?"

He removes the cigarette from his lips, reaches out the window, and grazes his thumb across the end, scattering ashes through the air. He takes another long drag and exhales before flicking the cigarette outside. Then he rolls up the window and wipes his damp hands on his jeans

"I can't go into the details just yet. All I can say is that I don't want to be working for your father, and after a while, I won't have to."

Something about his eyes warms the iciness that has possessed the inside of me for my entire life. So cold, yet so warm. So evil, yet appears so good. So much like me that it's frightening. Maybe if he can open up to me, I can open up to him. Tell him the truth about me. Tell him of my condition. Of what I did in the past. Maybe he wouldn't judge me.

"Be careful," I warn. "If my father knew you were saying what you are… He'd kill you."

Ryler's eyes blaze with passion. "I know that, but it's—you're worth the risk."

"I shouldn't be." My head tips forward so my hair is hiding the shame in my expression. "Not until you know the whole truth about me. That I'm just as dangerous as he is."

Ryler tangles his fingers through my hair, and tucks a few stray strands behind my ear. "Why do you say that?"

"Because," I whisper, shutting my eyes.

Don't speak, or I will cut off your tongue.

I'm so tired of being silent, though.

So tired.

Besides, if he knew I was crazy, then maybe he'd run.

Or maybe he wouldn't.

He did almost kill someone himself.

"I killed someone once," I admit.

Whether I can trust Ryler or not, it's too late. I've already divulged too much, and there's no going back.

I stare at my hands and flex my fingers, unable to look him in the eye. "It was in self-defense... But still, I have blood on my hands."

It grows so silent you can hear the rain splashing against the windows. Ryler cranks on the windshield wipers, but still doesn't drive forward.

"What did the man do to you?" he signs when I dare meet his gaze again. Astonishingly, he appears more curious than horrified. I wasn't expecting that kind of reaction.

"The guy I killed... He was raping a girl," I say, my voice unsteady. "His name was Defertoan. At least, that was his nickname. He was with that bodyguard Evan has, Taggers, the big guy with the hairy knuckles. They were both raping this girl, and then they came after me. Something snapped inside me, and instead of giving up, I fought back and ended up bashing a rock against Defertoan's head... He died."

Ryler's forehead creases. "Of course you wouldn't give up. Why would you say that?"

I lift my shoulders and shrug. "That's what I was taught to do. At least, when it comes to my father's world. Never fight back, talk back, or do anything other than obey. Of course, out in real world..." I bite down on my tongue. That's the second time I've almost let Ralingford slip out. Uttering the town's name would be the biggest mistake I've ever made, one I'm unsure I want to make yet. "You seem so surprised by the things I say. Just how far have you gone into Donny Elderman's world?"

He shakes his head, irritated. "Apparently not that far." He pauses, his puzzlement deepening. "What did they do to do you? I mean, after you killed Defertoan, how were you punished?"

I think about lying, but I've already gone headlong into this mess, so far submersed in the truth that before I know it, I'll probably be drowning. Literally. When my father finds out—because he always finds out—he'll drop me into the center of the lake with a weight strapped to my ankle and watch me drown.

I sweep my hair to the side and turn my back toward Ryler. With a trembling hand, I lift up the hem of my green velvet shirt. "He took a piece of me."

Ryler's breath catches in his throat. Moments later, his fingers brush across my side. His hand is shaking, and his uneasiness makes me warm inside. That might make me sound like a complete lunatic, but his shocked reaction means he's more human than most of Donny Elderman's men.

My heart beats five times before I lower my shirt and twist back around.

"What exactly did he do to you?" The anger blazing from Ryler's eyes startles me.

"He… He took my kidney." I close my eyes, remembering what it felt like when it happened. I was sedated, but awake, so I was aware of what was happening but couldn't feel anything.

Story of my life.

"Why would he do that? Just to punish you?"

"That, and my mother needed one. There was something wrong with hers, they were shutting down or something. The town doctor came and did surgery… gave her mine. The thing is, I probably would have agreed to do it if they'd asked." Maybe. Sometimes I wonder if I love my mother that much, which makes me a horrible person.

"I'm sorry that happened to you… the pain you must have gone through…" Ryler's jaw tightens as he absent-mindedly brushes a finger across the scar on his throat. "God, Emery, how could anyone do this to you?"

"Well, I did kill someone."

"In self-defense."

"But I wanted to kill him. I wanted to make him pay for hurting that girl and trying to hurt me." The truth is almost too much. "I think I might be like my father. I think killing came too naturally."

"No, I don't believe that at all. You're nothing like your father. At all. You're good and sweet and pure. You just haven't had a chance to be that person yet."

"I tried… When I came to Laramie, I was trying to be that person, but my old life followed me." The madness I ran from chased me down and seized hold of me again.

Ryler's lips part, but the vibration of a phone cuts him off. He offers me an apologetic look before reaching into his boot and retrieving his phone. His fingers move across the buttons, the screen illuminating through the darkness. It's just enough light to give me a glimpse of who he's texting.

My father.

I focus on the rain falling from the sky and drizzling down the windshield.

Truth and trust, they coincide. I've put a lot of trust in Ryler, spilled secrets people would kill me for.

Either it'll eventually set me free—he'll set me free.

Or it'll end up killing me

In the end, the choice is his.

Chapter 14

Deeper into the Rabbit Hole I Sink

Emery

We make the rest of the short drive to Evan's house in silence. Ryler doesn't tell me what my father texted him about, nor does he continue trying to get me to open up to him. He seems rather agitated, distracted, and remorseful. It has me concerned that perhaps he realized what a huge mistake it was prying me open like that.

Doesn't matter. What's done is done. And now I have to pay.

My heart aches inside my chest, though, and my body feels completely numb. I care about Ryler more than I've realized.

By the time we make it to Evan's, Ryler's demeanor changes from agitated to calm and composed. Ever since I found out Ryler works for my father, I've tried to figure out how I could have missed it. Seeing him interact with Evan, I'm starting to understand how I didn't know. Ryler is very good at being whoever he needs to be, and I worry that's exactly what he's done with me.

We're in the garage of the large house Evan has rented. Inside the home, there are a group of men who work with my father. They are stacking and counting packages of cocaine, and the scene reminds me of all the drugs I'd seen the night in Ralingford when I snuck out late that night. So many drugs and dealers, but that was only the tip of the iceberg. Inside the warehouse is where the experiments go on—where the drugs are tested. And, like the warehouses in Ralingford, Evan's home is set up with hundreds of alarms.

The garage must be the safety zone since we're free to move around. The space is bigger than my entire place, yet he doesn't have a single car parked inside. The concrete is stained with blood and oil. God knows what Evan's been doing in here.

Earlier today, he tried to convince me to move in with him again. I said no, but Evan has never been one to take no for an answer. Yes, yes, yes is all he'll accept. Anything less is unacceptable.

"You're going to do it, Emery," he said while his body was over mine. He'd been sticking his tongue down my throat until I denied his murmuring request to move in with him. "You and I are going to be together. Everyone wants this to happen."

Of course everyone wants it to happen. Your father and mine have wanted to merge our families since I was born, I wanted to say. Instead, I uttered, "I don't know if I'm ready for such a big, life-changing event."

"Well, you better get ready." His fingers pressed force-fully into my wrists, and I could actually feel my skin bruising. "I'm not going to wait around forever. And you know what your father will do if you refuse me."

My heart was thrashing so violently inside my chest that I thought I was going to have a panic attack and pass out right there in front of him, which would have been an irreversible mistake. Thankfully, he released me and left my apartment before that happened.

"This package is important." Evan's voice rips me from my thoughts. He's been pretending I don't exist. Some form of punishment for denying him, I'm sure. Really, it's a reward. "You know you're not supposed to open it," Evan reminds Ryler as he hands a small, square box to his bodyguard, Tagger, so he can give it to Ryler.

I'm sure the unnecessary exchange is because Evan thinks he's too good to make the exchange himself.

The three of them are completely different. Tagger is big, sturdy, and menacing. Evan looks like a walking poster of a lead singer in a boy band; blond hair, blue eyes, solid muscles, the perfect height. Dressed in black, facial piercings and tattoos, with messy black hair, Ryler is the opposite.

A mess because I ran my fingers through it. God, I hope Evan can't tell how attracted I am to Ryler. He'll kill him.

"Obviously," Ryler mouths to Evan as he takes the small package and tucks it into his pocket.

"I was just making sure you understood." Evan's gaze glides to my wrist before settling on my eyes. "Emery, you look more beautiful than ever today. Flushed by my presence, I'm sure."

Arrogant bastard.

The more time I spend with him, the more it feels like Evan is my jail sentence, my punishment for my sins. For killing. For being insane. For everything that I am.

When a sly grin spreads across Evan's face, my lip instinctively curls. Images of earlier today cut me like glass. How he pinned me to the bed and stuck his tongue down my throat, bit my lip hard as he rubbed against me. It's not the first time he's been that rough with me, and with the way things are going, I'm sure it won't be the last time either.

After being with Ryler, knowing what it's like to *want* a kiss, I feel more disgusted and used by Evan than I normally do. That disgust festers inside me, and I have the most overwhelming compulsion to claw Evan's eyes out.

The truth will set me free.

Maybe I'll just do it—claw his eyes out and let the truth kill me.

"What? No thank you?" The arch of his brow dares me to say something.

"Thank you," I mutter, balling my hands into fists. My fingernails pierce the flesh, split the skin open, and warm blood trickles inside my palm.

Ryler stiffens, his jaw ticks, and his face reddens with anger. I half expect him to lunge forward and punch Evan.

"We should go," Ryler signs to me, even though it looks like it's killing him to say it.

I nod, my rage matching his.

"We have to go," I pass Ryler's message along to Evan.

Evan glances back and forth between Ryler and me. Then without warning, he whisks forward, wraps an arm around my waist, and jerks my mouth to his. He tastes like onions and whiskey. So disgusting, just like his tongue in my mouth and the feel of his body against mine.

When he pulls away, he flashes me a grin. "I'll be stopping by tomorrow to talk more about you moving in." He starts to back away toward the door that leads to the inside of the house. "You better have an answer for me this time, Emery. I'm not a patient person, and you were raised to be the kind of girl who doesn't force me to be impatient. Your father put a lot of time and effort into making you the perfect person for me."

Ryler inches forward as his hands circle in the air. "She's not going to be home tomorrow. Doc's having me take her out of town."

Relief washes over me. That's news to me. But good news.

Evan pauses near the doorway. "What did he just say?" he asks me. "This is so ridiculous. I don't know why your father insists on letting a mute work for him."

Ryler cracks his knuckles and pops his neck. I can tell it's taking all of his restraint not to tackle Evan and beat him up. Part of me wants to remain silent and see if he'll end up giving in. Just like with the man I killed, part of me wants to see Evan suffer for his sins, even if it's at the cost of Ryler.

But the good side of me wins. The side that doesn't want to see anything bad happen to Ryler.

"He said I'm not going to be home tomorrow," I tell Evan then force a frown. "Sorry."

Evan's eyelids lower as he scowls at me. "That's not acceptable."

"My father's the one who told him," I say to Evan with a shrug. "So take it up with him."

Huffing in fury, Evan spins for the door with Tagger following at his heels. Seconds later, the door slams shut, and suddenly Ryler and I are alone in the garage.

We stare at each other for a few beats before Ryler sighs heavily and elevates his hands, "I lied about your father saying that."

My forehead creases. "You lied? Why?"

"Because you looked like you didn't want to meet him. And… And because he hurt you." He shrugs then reaches to tuck a strand of my hair behind my shoulder. "Emery, I care about you. I want you to know that."

I shiver from his touch, the good kind of shiver, the kind of shiver I hope means I can trust him. "Still, why would you do that? You know who Evan is, so I'm guessing you realize that he'll hurt you if he finds out. My father will be angry, too." I angle my chin downward and stare at the ground. "He wants this thing between Evan and me to happen more than anything else."

Ryler hooks a finger under my chin and angles my head back up. "I know."

I wet my chapped lips with my tongue. "Then why did you do it?"

"Because… I don't want to see you hurt anymore. And I'm going to do everything in my power to stop it."

"Well, thank you," I say, fully meaning it. The pressure on my chest cracks and shatters. Maybe this will turn out okay after all. "You didn't have to do that."

For a brief instant, everything feels perfect. Perfection does exist. Ryler is everything he says he is. Then the door to the house swings open, shattering the moment into a thousand pieces. Reality painfully seeps in as Evan comes storming back into the garage with a smirk on his face and two of his largest bodyguards at his heels.

"Just got a message from your father," he says, striding across the room toward me with even strides. His fingers are curled around an object, and I instantly shuffle back, not wanting to find out what he's holding.

Ryler steps in front of me and blocks me from Evan, but the bodyguards shove him back and grab him by the arms. He fights to get his arms free, but they push him against the wall while Evan snatches ahold of my arm.

His fingers roughly press against my skin, making the bruises on my flesh sting. "You've been telling our secrets, Emery, haven't you?"

"Of course not." I twist my arm, attempting to escape, but Evan tightens his grip.

"Thou shall not speak of the stuff inside Ralingford," he breathes hotly against my face. "Your father tried to warn you. Tried to scare you into going home. You should have listened to the notes, Emery, because now you're in this on your own."

"I knew the notes were from him," I hiss, losing all my self-control. "I fucking knew he was doing that to try to get me out of my place."

Evan flinches, stunned by my outburst. His shock swiftly vanishes, though, and rage possesses his face.

"You. Will. Not. Speak. To. Me. That. Way." With his free hand, he strikes me across the face so hard my ears ring.

Ryler head-butts one of the bodyguards and ends up getting punched in the stomach. He grunts and collapses to his knees with the two large men still restraining him by the arms. They drag him back into the corner and start punching him.

"Stop hurting him!" I cry, my voice and words echoing around us.

I've said this before, in the same manner, been in almost the same position. Only instead of Ryler, it was Ellis. I couldn't see him, but his cries filled the house as my father punished him. And all I did was watch. Watched him suffer because I was afraid.

But no more.

I'm going to be free.

It's time.

Time to run away.

"You had no right to tell him who I am," Evan growls, jerking me closer to him. Our faces are so close our foreheads touch, and his breath is hot against my cheek. "And speaking ill of your father like that, betraying the man who raised you… What kind of a daughter are you?"

I have no clue what's going on. How on earth did my father and Evan find out what I told Ryler? Yes, I expected that it might happen if Ryler chose to tell my father, but if he did, how could he have done it so quickly? There's no way Ryler had time to tell them unless…

I grind my teeth until my jaw pulsates in pain. Unless that's what he was doing in the car when he was texting my father.

No, he wouldn't do that.

Or would he?

I don't know.

I'm so confused.

Drowning in madness.

Never to breathe again.

No, I won't go down like this.

I'm going to fight.

"Now you have to pay." Evan raises his hand between us, his fingers wrapped around a syringe.

"I won't be punished again!" I shout, wrenching my arm away while bringing my knee up to kick him. "The scar on my side is enough. I've paid enough."

My foot collides with Evan's shin, and his fingers slip from my arm as he lets out a sequence of curses. I skitter around him and sprint toward the open door leading into the house, but one of the bodyguards clotheslines me with his arm and my legs flip out from under me.

I collapse to the ground, and my head hits the concrete as the world starts to spin in bright colors and odd shapes. My neck throbs in pain as my lungs battle to get oxygen.

"I tried to warn you," Ellis' voice fills my head. "I'm so sorry, Emery. I knew they were coming for you, just like they did with me."

Evan appears above me, red faced and enraged. For the first time since we met, he doesn't seem so beautiful. He seems ugly and horrid. Flaws, flaws, flaws for the entire world to see.

"I hate you," I choke out as he snatches ahold of my arm. "And one day, I'm going to make you pay for this."

"That's a big threat for such a hollow, pathetic girl." He plunges the needle into my forearm.

Like a match struck, my veins ignite with white-hot pain. "No… I'm… going… to… be… free…

"No, you won't," Evan says through my cries, smiling, smiling, smiling, as if he's wholly enjoying my pain. "No matter what you want, you'll still end up with me, Emery. Your life has never been your own. My plans for our future together will happen. Now, down, down the rabbit hole you go."

My flesh scorches like melting wax as I'm dragged into the darkness of my own mind.

Down, down the rabbit hole indeed.

Chapter 15

The Secrets of Butterflies are About to Fly Free

Ryler

The instant Emery slips into unconsciousness, Evan's bodyguards free me from their hold. I stumble from my knees and stride across the garage, heading straight for Evan, ready to slam my fist into his face.

"I wouldn't do that if I were you," he warns as he straightens his legs and stands up. He has the syringe in his hand and a pleased grin on his face. "You know who I am now; therefore, I'm pretty sure you can guess the consequences of so much as laying a finger on me."

Even though it kills me, I grind to a halt. If I go after him, his bodyguards are going to kill me. Revenge can't go down like this. It has to be more discreet. But it's going to happen.

201

"What was that?" I mouth to Evan.

"Just a little drug my father invented," he says, eyeing me over. "Don't worry. It didn't kill her. It has a little bit of heroin in it, so she'll be out for a while. But she should wake up in a few hours as good as new." He starts for the door again, but pauses at the steps. "Although, her mind might be a little out of whack. At least, that's what happens in most of the patients my father tested the drug on."

My eyes widen. *Wait, what?*

He rolls his eyes. "Don't worry. It's only short-term. Just long enough for her to learn her lesson to keep her fucking mouth shut."

My fingers curl into fists. What I wouldn't do to be able to beat the shit out of him, but like with Ben, if I hit Evan, things aren't going to go in my favor. I need to be careful, yet still bring that fucking asshole down.

Evan glances at Emery lying on the floor, then looks over at his bodyguards. "Put her in the car," he orders. "Doc said to let Ryler drive her home." He seems irked as hell about that.

Like fucking hell they're touching her.

Shoving him out of the way, I stride across the garage and bend over to pick up Emery. Without mouthing a word, I lift her into my arms and carry her past Evan and to the door.

"I said to let my bodyguards carry her out," he calls out, chasing after me.

Ignoring him, I hurry out of the garage, through the house, and out the front door. When I get to the driveway, I gently put Emery in the passenger seat of my car and check her vitals before heading around to hop in the car. Evan is exiting his house by the time I have the driver's side door open.

"Did you just deliberately disobey me?" he asks from the front porch, while his bodyguards linger in the door-way.

Battling the urge to rush over and slam my fist into his face, I lower my head to climb in.

He runs off the steps and grabs the door as I move to shut it. "I know you can't speak, but I know you can hear. You weren't supposed to touch Emery. My guards were supposed to put her in the car. Not you."

I count to ten backwards in my head. His guards are distracted by something inside. They're not paying attention. I could beat the shit out of him right now and peel out of here before they get to me. But then what about consequences?

Calm. Stay calm. You'll only make the situation worse if you don't.

Evan smirks at me like he's won some sort of battle. "As soon as she wakes up, let me know so I can come fuck the shit out of her and remind her who's in control."

That's it. Something snaps inside me—all of my control. I hop out of the car with my elbow craned back. Before he can react, I bash my fist into his nose.

He stumbles back, cursing, as he cups his nose. "You fucking—"

I cut him off with a punch to the gut and then counter the move, my knuckles colliding with his ribcage. I steal one last hit to his jawline before bailing out, because the guards have taken notice.

They holler at me as I dive back into my car and slam the door. Then I drive like mad down the road, constantly

checking in my rearview mirror to see if I'm being followed. I'm not sure how this is going to go. Is Evan going
to come after me himself? It seems doubtful. More than
likely he'll send someone else.

So what do I do next? I could call Doc and try to explain, but from what Evan said, Doc is the reason he
injected Emery. Plus, he's the one who's been sending her
those notes to scare her. No wonder he knew about the last
note the moment Emery received it, despite the fact that
Emery never brought it up.

Another question plaguing me is how in the hell did
Doc find out that Emery told me he is a monster, and Evan
is Donny Elderman's son? How does he seem to know everything the moment it happens? It doesn't make any sense.

I need to text Stale and tell him Evan is Donny's son.
Then let him know what I've done before I get the fuck out
of here.

Shit, this is so bad. I should feel pissed off at myself
for making the same mistake again, for losing control and
retaliating with violence.

I glance at Emery leaning against the car door, completely out of it, just as powerless as me. No, I don't feel angry at all for protecting her. It was worth it. I just wish I knew how to protect us both now.

Fuck! This isn't fair. She shouldn't have to go through this all because I pushed her to open up to me. I never should have brought her tonight. I had a bad feeling but went against my gut. All so I could what? Pick up another stupid package. Stay on Doc's good side?

With one hand on the steering wheel, I yank the package out of my pocket. It seems too small to be carrying drugs. I've never bothered looking inside the packages I'm supposed to deliver. Usually it's all about business, but after what they did to Emery tonight, I want to know what's in it—what I'm doing this for.

Carefully lifting the lid off the box, I peek inside.

What the hell?

My gaze snaps to Emery. Her arm is lying lifelessly to her side. Attached to her wrist is a silver bracelet with a butterfly pendant shimmering against the glow of the streetlights filtering through the window. It's the exact same bracelet that's in the box except Emery's is secured by a twist tie. I've noticed her wearing it before, but it has never been broken. Is that what this package is for? A replacement? Or is it something more?

I flip over the bracelet in the box and squint at the inscription on the back of the butterfly pendant. *So we'll always know where you are.*

A tracking device? Is that what this is? Is that how her father seems to always know what she's doing?

Things are starting to make sense.

I put the lid back on the box, stuff it into my pocket, and race to get home, breaking every traffic law. By the time I park the car, it's past five o'clock in the morning and the sun is clipping the peaks of the shallow mountains. I'm exhausted and confused, but I've calmed down enough to come up with a plan. Carry Emery upstairs then text Stale and let him know what's happened, see if he knows what's wrong with Emery. See if he thinks I should take her to the hospital, and what he thinks I should do now that I've beaten the shit out of Evan.

My "business" phone suddenly buzzes in my pocket, and my fingers fumble as I fish it out.

Doc: You've really messed up, Ryler. I'm disappointed you let my daughter get to you like that. I warned you not to let her. Stay put. I'm headed there to pick her up and punish you accordingly.

Fuck. I have about an hour before he shows up, and I need to make sure I'm long gone before that happens.

I turn off the engine, jump out of the car into a rain puddle, and hurry to the passenger side. I open the door, scoop up Emery in my arms, and hurry up the stairway. When I make it into her apartment, I set her down on the sofa, then race down the stairway to my apartment. The place is silent except for faint snoring coming from Luke and Violet's bedroom. I move as quietly as I can, rushing to my bedroom, shut the door, and dig out my "personal" phone.

Me: I found out Evan is Donny Elderman's son. Did you know about this? Also, he injected Emery with some sort of drug tonight that made her pass out. He said something about it making her mind go out of whack??? Have any idea what it is? He said it had a lit-

tle heroin in it. Oh, and I don't know how, but it seems like Evan knew stuff that Emery told me privately...

Stale: I'm not sure about the drugs, but Donny's been known for making experimental street drugs, so my guess is he injected her with one of those. Are her vitals okay?

Me: Yeah, but I think I should maybe take her to the hospital.

Stale: Make sure you're absolutely sure before you do anything. We don't want to risk your cover being blown. And if she's on heroin, she could get in some trouble.

Cover being blown. Like that fucking matters right now.

Stale: And we've had our suspicions about Evan already. But we have no positive confirmation on his identity yet since there are no records of a birthdate or even a social security number linked to him. We figured he was just another nameless person Donny picked up off the street... How did you get this information?

Me: Emery let it slip. And somehow Evan knew she'd told me, even though we were in Emery's apartment with no one around. It makes no sense. I know Doc is the one finding out all this stuff, but I can't figure out who's telling him.

Stale: I'm going to look into Evan. Do some more background searching to see if I can link him directly to Donny Elderman. If he is his son, we could bring him in. He'd know where his father's warehouse is.

Me: It's not going to be that easy. He always has bodyguards around him. Tons. And I'm pretty sure they've got the entire house set up with some sort of high-tech alarm system. Plus, I doubt he'll talk even if you bring him in. You know they brand silence into their kids pretty well.

Stale: You leave Evan for me to worry about. In the meantime, keep working on Emery. And be very careful. From what you said about Doc knowing things that have barely happened, I'm guessing that it's not someone who's relaying the information to him, but something. My bet is that Emery's house is bugged, which either means Doc doesn't trust you or doesn't trust his daughter.

My fingers fold tightly around the phone. *Shit, this is so bad.*

Me: Not sure that's my biggest problem now since I beat the shit out of Evan about a half an hour ago.

Stale: You did what? Tell me you're joking.

Me: Nope. And Doc is heading here now to punish me, and then he's taking Emery back home. I have about an hour before he gets here. I need to run.

Stale: Don't run. We need to get you out of there safely. Fuck, Ryler. You really fucked this up. God-dammit.

Me: Yeah, I know, but I had to do what I had to do. And I'm not going anywhere without Emery.

Stale: Emery's not your problem. And we still might be able to use her. You said Doc is taking her back home. Maybe we can follow them.

Me: No way. I'm not going to let that happen.

Stale: This isn't your choice anymore. Stay put. Someone will be there soon.

Someone will be there soon. What does that even mean? I'm not about to wait around to find out.

Shoving the phone into my pocket, I rush back up to Emery's apartment. The moment I step foot into her living room, I know something's wrong. The lights are off when I left them on, and Emery is no longer on the sofa. I reach behind me to grab her gun still tucked in the waistband of my jeans, but before I can grab the weapon, someone rams me from the side. The force is minimal, and I easily regain my footing.

I whip out the gun and whirl in the direction of the figure. The moonlight shines through the sliding glass door across the room and highlights the perfectly structured features of the person who attacked me.

My jaw drops. *Emery.*

Before I can process what's happening, she charges at me again. Not wanting her to fall and hurt herself, I allow her body to crash into mine. The impact sends me stumbling backward into the coffee table. We both hit the ground, the gun flying out of my hand. I flip to my stomach and push myself up, but Emery is already standing.

I think about the drug Evan said he gave her, and how when she woke up, her mind might be a little out of whack. I need to communicate with her, see if she's coherent or not, but I need the lights on in order to do so.

I sidestep and reach for the light, but she charges me again. Her head rams into my stomach, and we go tumbling down the hallway, bumping into the wall before landing on the floor with her on top of me. That stupid wooden decoration falls to the floor, and a bright red light starts flashing.

Shit, is that where the bug is? No wonder I've always had a bad feeling about the thing.

Emery is wild above me as she tries to scratch my face with her fingernails. It's like she's lost her mind on a bad trip. Then she notices the light and freezes with her hands on my shoulders and her eyes fixated on the broken object.

"He's going to kill me," she whispers, and then her body slumps on top of mine.

I slide out from under her, trying not to panic as I check her pulse. Her heartbeat has quickened, and her skin looks pallid against the limited moonlight flowing through the windows.

Pushing to my feet, I reach for the light switch, but then stop myself. My gut instinct is telling me not to turn on the light and to get the fuck out of this house. This time I'm going to listen.

Crouching down, I yank the bracelet from her wrist and chuck it aside, along with the package I picked up tonight. Then I slide my hands under her, carefully scoop her into my arms, and carry her out the door and downstairs to my apartment.

Once I reach my bedroom, I kneel down beside my bed and lay her down on the mattress. Long locks of her hair are sprawled across my pillow and her arm is resting over her stomach. Her skin still looks pale, her lips are red, and every once in a while her eyelashes flutter.

I sit down on the edge of the bed and watch her chest rise and fall with each breath, growing angrier and angrier over what's happening. I've had a really shitty life. My parents were assholes. My foster parents were assholes. My one and only girlfriend was an asshole. But it feels like Emery has had it way worse. Tortured and abused, those

214

are the two words that come to mind when I think of her. The dying rose I described can barely thrive and the petals will all be gone soon. No one will ever be able to see them anymore. I won't be able to see them anymore.

Even though she's Doc's daughter, she's just as much a victim as everyone else Donny Elderman and his men have annihilated. I can't believe that, only hours ago, I was actually considering using her to get to the warehouse, using this already broken girl.

I brush my finger across her cheek; her face instinctively nuzzles against my touch, and she murmurs my name. Something breaks inside me, something I've been fighting to keep together since the first time I met her. I make a vow right then and there to make sure Emery stays out of this mess. That no matter what it takes, I'll get her out of this life.

Pushing to my feet, I dig my "personal" phone out of my pocket. The lack of hesitation I feel when I send the text makes me feel pretty content with my choice, regardless of the consequences.

Me: I'm going to tell Emery everything, and then I'm going to leave and take her with me.

Chapter 16

Lost Days . . . Again

Emery

Clank. Clank. Clank.

"You made me do this," my father says, his voice drifting up the stairway to the kitchen. Clank. Clank. Clank. "I have to do this because of you."

"What's Father doing down there?" I ask my mother, staring at the closed door of the basement. My arms are strapped to the kitchen chair, and my ankles are bound to the legs. Ever since I snuck out of the house, I've been tied up except for when I go to school.

Clank. Clank. Clank.

"How dare you ask such questions." My mother takes a seat across from me and grasps the pendant dangling

around her neck. "You know better than to question any-thing your father does."

Clank. Clank. Clank.

"I'm sorry things turned out this way, son," my father mutters. "But in the end, I think it's for the best. Now the darkness no longer stains your soul."

Clank. Clank. Clank.

My mother winces then twists the cap on the pendant. Removing it, she puts it up to her nose and sucks up the white powder. Her nostrils are ringed with red and a glimmer of red flashes from the silver metal of the pendant.

"What's that?" I ask, nodding my head at the pendant. "That light."

"That is for your father to keep track of me," she replies, her words rushed together as she sniffs a few times

"You're not supposed to be doing that." I don't know why I say it. Perhaps it's the clanking. Perhaps it's because deep down I know what's happening in the basement. Or maybe it's just because I'm crazy.

Her pupils dilate as she leans across the table and strikes me hard. "How dare you speak to me like that." She pushes the chair back from the table, walks around to me, and bends down. With a flick of her fingers, she unties the binds around my ankles then rises to her feet and frees my wrists.

"Thank you," I tell her, stunned.

She smirks. "Now maybe your father will do to you what he's done to my son, then I'll no longer have to worry anymore." With that, she leaves the room.

Clank. Clank. Clank.

I know I should go up to my room, stay away from the basement, but my legs lift me from the seat and take me in the direction of the clanking. I turn the doorknob and pad down the concrete stairs. The surface is cold against my bare feet and the air is arctic, like midnight during wintertime.

Clank. Clank. Clank.

I reach the bottom of the stairway and see my father standing there with a shovel in his hand. The concrete of the floor has been torn up in one area, exposing the dirt beneath it. Beside the hole is my brother, sprawled across the ground. His arms are lifeless, his legs are bent in an awkward way, and his skin is a pale blue.

Clank. Clank. Clank.

"Emery, you're not supposed to be down here," my father says calmly as he continues to dig.

"I'm sorry." I step back to head upstairs, unable to remove my gaze from Ellis.

"You might as well help, now that you're down here." My father stabs the shovel into the dirt.

"I..." I trail off as Ellis turns his head toward me.

His eyes are wide and his lips parted. "Help me," *he mouths.*

When I blink, his head is turned the other way, and he's no longer moving. I'm not sure if what I saw was real, but I want to help him.

"He can't breathe," I whisper in horror.

"Emery, grab a shovel and help me dig," my father demands, pointing at a shovel leaning against the wall. "And stop whining." When I don't answer, he bashes the

shovel against the wall, missing my head by inches. "Help me or else join your brother."

My body trembles as I skitter across the room while my father continues to dig.

Clank. Clank. Clank.

My fingers wrap around the wooden handle. I feel so cold inside as I turn back around. My eyes immediately drop to Ellis's body. I don't want to do this.

His eyes are still open and his lips move again. "Then don't. Let your mind take you somewhere else."

I suck in a breath and shut my eyes. Everything around me fades away.

I'm familiar with drugs as much as my lungs are familiar with air, my body with blood, my wrists with restraints, and my mind with hallucinations. When Evan plunged that needle into my arm, I knew I was going to go under for at least a couple of days. That's the way it always is with Donny's experimental drugs. I saw firsthand that night I snuck out what kind of damage his drugs do to people. All those people living on the rundown side of town were malnourished, out of their minds, and tortured by their addiction Donny was intent on feeding.

Still, even knowing what happened to me—that I was dropped into some sort of high—when I open my eyes, the panic sets in.

I'm awake.

I'm awake.

I'm awake.

What happened?

What happened?

What happened?

I bolt upright in a bed, but immediately regret it as my head pounds. "God… how long this time?" I mutter as I scan my surroundings.

An unmade bed that's not mine, a table and chair, a television, and a single window with the curtain drawn shut. Dust lines the orange carpet, and the walls are stained. I'm in a cheap motel room.

"How did I get here?" I fling the blankets off my body and cringe at the sight of the T-shirt and boxer shorts I'm wearing that definitely don't belong to me, and my bracelet is gone.

The latter is a relief. After remembering what my mother said about her own pendant—about it being so my father could keep track of her—I worry mine may serve the same purpose. Still, I wonder how I forgot about it… And how I forgot about my brother.

Ellis, I'm so sorry.

I rack my brain for an image of how I got here, perhaps an image containing blood staining my hands or with my fingers wrapped around the handle of a shovel. The last time something like this happened was the night I saw my brother dead… God, how could I have forgotten what I did to him? How I helped bury him.

"I'm so sorry I forgot about you," I whisper, sucking back the tears. "I really am."

"You did what you had to do," Ellis's voice fills my thoughts. *"Don't worry, I forgive you. It wasn't your fault. You need to let me go."*

I think about how I see him all the time, how I talk to him—talk to the dead. It should mean I'm crazy, but at the moment, I feel strangely sane, like my mind has found inner peace.

Still, I have to wonder what's real and what isn't.

"Is this real?" I ask myself, peering around the motel room. "The last thing I remember is being drugged."

Silence is my only response. Unsure of what else to do, I check my arms for more injection sites, but only spot the one, which has faded to a yellowish bruise. I reach for the hem of my shirt and lift it up to check my body for fresh wounds. Other than the faint traces of a few bruises, everything appears to be intact. I release a breath and stand to my feet. My legs shake like two wet noodles as I stumble for the door. After unlatching the deadbolt, I reach for the doorknob, but before I can turn it, the door swings open.

I trip backward and bump into the wall as a man a bit younger than my father walks in, carrying a cup of coffee. He's wearing a white button-down shirt with a loosened red tie around the collar. His slacks have a stain on them, and his shoes look a little worn.

He startles when he sees me, but quickly composes himself. "Oh, good, you're awake."

I skitter away from him, but my feet are still figuring out how to work again, and I end up tripping into the dresser.

"Easy," the man says, raising his free hand up. "I'm not here to hurt you. I'm here to help you."

I grip on to the corner of the dresser as I fight to keep my legs underneath me. "That's what they all say." My voice is scratchy, and my throat feels like sandpaper. I cough, trying to clear it.

The man slowly shuts the door then extends the coffee toward me. "Here, you probably need this more than me."

I shake my head. "Do you think I'm stupid?" I ask, eyeing the cup as if it's the enemy. "I just woke up from being drugged. I'm not about to let it happen again."

He glances down at the cup with his brows knit, then he must realize something because I see something click in his eyes. "Right. I get it. Trust, right?" He raises the cup to his lips and takes as sip, watching my reaction over the rim. "See, perfectly drug free."

"Nothing is perfect," I tell him, taking a few more steps back. The world spins around me, and I stop, realizing that I don't have anywhere to go. "Who are you? And where am I?"

He sighs and moves to set the cup of coffee on the table. "It's there if you change your mind." He pulls out a chair and sinks down in it. "This was never supposed to happen," he mumbles, rubbing his hand across his face. "If he would have just followed the damn rules," he shakes his head and lowers his hand, huffing out a breath, "none of this would have happened."

"Tell me who you are," I demand, cringing at the quiver in my voice. Fear is seeping out of me, giving me away.

"You don't need to be afraid of me," he says in a gentle tone. "I'm not here to hurt you."

I flatten my back to the wall and keep my eyes trained on him like a hawk. "How about you tell me who you are and let me decide that for myself. Are you… Do you work for my father? Or are you one of his enemies?"

"Neither." He mutters something under his breath again and curses about a thousand times. "I'm Federal Agent Stale. I work for the FBI."

My lips part in shock. Not at all what I was expecting. "I don't… no you can't…" I shake my head. "You're lying."

He sticks his hand into the pocket of his pants and retrieves a leather wallet. Then he stands from the chair, opens the wallet, and shows me the silver metal inside—his badge.

I stare at it disbelief. "Am I hallucinating again?"

His face contorts in confusion. "Do you do that a lot?"

"I…" I'm struck speechless. When Evan had injected me with the drug, I never expected to wake up with an FBI agent. And where the hell is Ryler?

I scan the room, searching for signs of him, my clothes, my phone, anything belonging to my old life, but it's like it's—I've—been erased. I veer toward a panic attack, my breathing turning ragged as my pulse soars through the roof.

227

"Emery, I promise I'm not going to hurt you," the agent says, concerned. "In fact, I'm here to help you."

"Help me with what?" I gasp for air, inching back, but I'm already backed up to the wall. I have nowhere to go. "No one can help me anymore."

"That's not true. I promise I can help you."

I narrow my eyes. "Sure you can, but only for a price, right? Isn't that the way things go?"

He tensely massages the back of his neck. "I'm not going to lie to you." His arm falls to the side, and he straightens his stance. "I do want something from you, but you have my word that you'll be protected if you give me what I want."

"I have your word." A sharp laugh escapes my lips. "I don't even know you, and yet you just what? Expect me to trust you."

"Yes."

"Well, I don't."

A contemplative look crosses his face. "Aren't you curious about what I want?"

"No." I inch toward the window, putting distance between us.

"Why not?"

"Because I already know what you want." I spring for the window and reach out to open it, but it doesn't even have a latch.

"How on earth can you possibly know what I want?" he asks from behind me, sounding as calm as can be.

I whirl around and face him. Panic swims through my veins as my vision spots in and out of focus. "Do you think I'm stupid?" I blink to hold onto reality, fight not to let my panic attack get the best of me.

He gapes at me. "No, not at all. Why would you say that?"

"Because you asked me if I know why I'm here. Of course I do. I know who I am, where I come from, so when a federal agent shows up in my life, I'm pretty sure I know the reason behind it."

"Oh, well, then good. I don't have to explain it to you." He offers me a warm smile, and I swallow hard.

Something still doesn't feel right.

"I still don't know why I'm in this room, though," I point out, leaning against the wall, "instead of at a police station. And I'm not sure how I got here."

"That's because this entire situation has become extremely complicated." He pauses. "And kind of dangerous."

"Everything is always complicated and dangerous," I tell him. "That's life."

He sighs then returns to his chair and motions to the bed. "Sit down and I'll explain a few things to you. Hopefully, we can clear up some of your confusion."

I eye the door then the bed.

"I'm not going to hurt you," he says, reading my silence.

"I know you aren't going to physically hurt me." I remain motionless for a few more minutes, while the detective patiently waits for me to make up my mind. Finally, seeing no other alternative, I cross the room and sit down on the bed. "Why am I here in a motel room?"

"Because the police station isn't a safe place for you to be," he replies without missing a beat. "Bringing you here was the only alternative."

"Why isn't it safe? Are the police corrupt?" I wouldn't be surprised with how powerful Donny Elderman is. "Are you corrupt?" I ask, realizing how easily he could be working for Donny or my father.

The detective shakes his head. "No, I'm not corrupt. I'm the opposite of corrupt." He reclines back in the seat and props his foot up on his knee. "Besides, corruptness isn't the reason you're not at the station."

"Then what is the reason?" I aim to sound firm, calm, and steady as a rock, but I'm a nervous wreck, and it shows through my off-pitch voice.

"Because we have someone you know there," he answers, watching me closely. "And we found it necessary to make sure the two of you aren't near each other for the time being."

My breath hitches in my throat. Ryler? What if he's been arrested? He was the last person with me. At least, from what I can remember.

The detective rests his arms along the armrest of the chair. "Tell me how much you know about Evan Elderman."

My heart slams against my chest so forcefully that I choke. He used the name Evan Elderman, not his fake name, Evan Moleney.

"I don't know who you're talking about," I reply indifferently, my pulse soaring through the roof.

"Yes, you do." He reaches for the coffee, takes a swallow, and then continues, "Maybe you recognize him by the name Evan Moleney."

I grip the edge of the bed to keep from falling because it feels like I'm tumbling, down, down the rabbit hole, right where Evan sent me. "Is this a test?"

Shock masks the detective's face. "What?"

I glance at the mirror on the wall. "Is there someone watching us through that, seeing how much information I'll divulge?"

He stares at me like I've lost my mind. "I don't know what you're talking about, Emery. That's just a mirror, and this is just a motel room. Nothing more."

I leap from the bed, my mind racing a million miles a minute. This is all wrong. I'm still being punished— tested—to see if I'll spill more secrets. "I won't tell you anything." I tug my fingers through my hair, yanking at the roots. I never should have opened my mouth. *Ever.* I'm going to end up like Ellis, buried in the basement, never to be found.

But maybe that's what I deserve for all the sins I've committed.

"Shit," the detective curses, jumping to his feet. "Emery, please calm down. This isn't what you think it is."

My head whips in his direction. "How could you possibly know what I think this is?"

His hands are in front of him as he approaches me like I'm a skittish cat. "Because I know who your father is… know some of the stuff that's been done to you. You've been hurt. A lot. But you need to understand that I'm not here to hurt you. You're safe now. Everything's going to be fine."

For every step he takes toward me, I counter his movement, backing myself toward the door. "How could you possibly know anything about me unless you work for my father? It doesn't make any sense."

"You've never told anyone what's happened to you before? No one at all?" His pressing gaze conveys insinuation.

Ryler. My lips remained sealed, even though I think the detective might already know the answer to his question.

He blows out a frustrated breath. "How can I get you to trust me? Tell me what I need to do, because I really want to earn your trust, Emery."

I bite at my fingernails, glancing around the room. Trust. I've only vaguely trusted one person in my entire life. "I want… I want to talk to Ryler. Do you… Do you know who he is?"

He warily nods. "Of course I know who he is."

"Good. Can you tell him to come here?" My gaze lands on the phone on the nightstand. "Or better yet, give me my phone and I'll text him. He's the only one I feel like I can trust right now."

"I can't give you your phone just yet."

My gaze lands on him again. "Why not?"

He scratches the top of his head and then sighs. "Because Ryler works for me, and if he has any contact with you at the moment, he's going to end up dead."

Chapter 17

My Salvation

Emery

A panic attack hits me like a ravenous storm. The clouds roll over me in the snap of a finger and adrenaline drowns me and soaks me to the bone. I collapse to the floor and land on my knees, the carpet scraping at my skin.

All this time, he was a lie.

Just like I always wondered.

Yet, he wasn't the lie I thought.

He was the opposite.

And now I have no idea how to feel.

Not a damn clue.

I want to be angry.

But I can't find the anger inside me.

All I feel is relief.

"What do you mean he works for you?" I whisper through my gasps. If I don't get myself under control, I'm going to black out. "Ryler works for my father… He works for Donny."

"No, he doesn't." The detective crouches in front of me and levels his gaze with mine. "He's worked for me as an informant even before he came to Laramie. He's been trying to find the location of Donny Elderman's warehouse so we can bring Donny down."

I slump back against the dresser and hug my knees to my chest. Breathe in. Breathe out. "That's what this is about? Bringing Donny's warehouse down?"

"It's part of it." He sits down on the floor, crisscrossing his legs. "I think you know how bad of a man Donny is. If we were able to find him and arrest him, all the stuff that goes on in those warehouses would end."

I shake my head and give him a *really* look. "You can't possibly believe that. His men would continue his work even if he is gone. He'd probably get off easy, too, with all the connections he has.

"He'd continue all his drug experiments. No matter what, his business would remain and innocent people would continue being test subjects for his drug experiments."

"Some of that might be true, but it might not. And in the process of arresting Elderman, we'd have a chance to detain a lot of his men," he says, resting back on his hands. "Those warehouses—that *town* you lived in—would be gone."

I elevate my chin and hold his gaze. "So that's what this is about? Finding the town? The grown man everyone fears?"

"Not everyone fears him," he replies. "Otherwise, no one would be after him."

"That's not true. Everyone fears him in their own way. And fear grows in the dirt of that town, soaks the air, is engrained into the minds of every single person who resides there. That's how a place like that exists. Without fear, the society would crumble."

He studies me carefully. "You're an insightful girl," he finally says with his head tilted. "I wasn't expecting that."

"You say insightful, most say crazy," I mutter, which only deepens his puzzlement.

He stares for a moment or two before saying, "Well, my main focus is finding Donny Elderman, not the town. The man has been off the radar for years, yet he's toxic to the country." He loosens his tie more, wipes the sweat from his brow, and then rests back on his hands. "But yes, I'd like to bring the town down in the process. From what I understand, there are hundreds of citizens being forced as subjects to his drug experiments. There are no rules, no laws to abide by because no one knows it exists. Regardless, if that restriction and control is based on fear, like you say, a place like that shouldn't exist. "

"Why do you care so much?" I wonder, resting my chin on my knee. "Some people usually turn their heads for the right amount of money. Or has no one tried to buy you off yet?"

"No, there have been a few who have tried to buy my silence, but that's not who I am," he insists. "I believe that we need to bring the place down."

I fold my arms and rest back against the dresser behind me. "*We*? Who said anything about me helping you? I never agreed to that."

He assesses me and I mimic his move, surprised by my spout of newfound confidence.

"According to Ryler, you're a good, trustworthy person, which would make you the kind of person who wants to help with something like this." When I don't say anything, he straightens his legs and rises to his feet. "Guess Ryler was wrong." He fishes his phone from his pocket and dials a number. "Doesn't matter, though. Now that we have Evan Elderman detained, we can still make this happen."

I'm not positive if he's telling the truth. The idea that the police somehow managed to arrest Evan seems impossible. "Even if that's true." I bend my legs and stand to my feet. "Even if you have Evan, he'll never tell you anything. He was taught not to open his mouth about his father's secrets, and unlike me, Evan will do anything to take his secrets to the grave. He's not weak like me."

The detective pauses then hangs up the phone. "Unlike you? Does that mean you'll help us?"

I think about all my confessions to Ryler, how amazing it felt to get the years of lies and sins off my chest. I think of Ellis buried in the basement, forgotten, even by me. Perhaps telling the truth could be my salvation. Ellis said the truth would set me free, and I owe him that much—owe him the truth.

"I'd need to know I was safe first." I sink down on the mattress. "After this… I'll never be able to live a normal life, especially in Laramie."

He sits down near the foot of the bed a few feet away from me. "You can live a normal life, but you're right. You won't be able to live in Laramie. We can set you up someplace safe, give you a new name and identity. A new life, if that's what you want."

What he's saying sounds wonderful. I want it so much my body aches and pleads to be free from the invisible restraints always controlling me. But could it be this easy? I'm still a bit skeptical.

"Are you talking about witness protection?" I ask the detective.

He nods. "I am."

I stare at the backs of my hands. My fingernails are chipped and my skin is dry. I'm falling apart on the outside, yet I don't mind. With each part of my appearance that breaks, I feel so much more like myself, a person I haven't fully discovered, but want to more than I want anything else.

My hands drop to my lap. "There's more that I want other than protection."

"I figured as much." He stuffs his phone into the front pocket of his shirt.

Mustering all the confidence I have, I square my shoulders. "When you raid the town, I want you to go to my house—I'll give you the address if you need it. When you get there, I want you to arrest my mother along with my father. Both of them need to be put in jail if this is going to happen... My mother has a," I make air quotes, "pharmacy she runs and gives people drugs, so charges against her shouldn't be a problem. If that doesn't work, check her necklace. She keeps cocaine in there."

I suck in a breath, then another, yet I can't feel the air saturating my lungs. "Underneath the basement floor of my house are the bones of my brother. I want them exhumed, and I want him to be given a proper burial." His jaw drops at that request, but I keep going, needing to get all my secrets out. "And finally, I want to be set up with a psychia-psychiatrist wherever I end up. I need to find out… Well, what's wrong with me." If I'm crazy or not. If I have psychosis or what. Who I really am when I'm not under the power of my mother and father.

"Why do you think something's wrong with you?"

"That's for me to worry about, not you. And there's one last request that I want as well. If you agree to all of this, then I'll give you what you want."

He grows fidgety. "What's the final request?"

I inhale and exhale. Inhale. Exhale. Breathe. Breathe. Breathe. Because that's all I can do.

"I want to see Ryler before I go to wherever you're sending me. I want to say goodbye." And I want to say I'm sorry for being who I am. He was the good guy all along, yet I treated him as if he were as wicked as me.

I rub my hand over my tender chest. It hurts thinking about leaving him behind, when it feels like we're just starting. In the end, I know I have to leave to get my beginning, to get a chance at ever having a normal life.

The detective considers my offer for a small amount of time before standing to his feet. He holds up a finger as he fishes his phone from his pocket again and dials a number. He wanders toward the door with the receiver pressed to his ear.

I begin to grow worried about who he's calling and wish I had a better grasp on reality so I could know, *know* that all of this is real. That soon, I could finally, *finally* be free. Sure, I'll be someone else, with a different name. I might even have to cut my hair. Honestly, I'm perfectly okay shedding my so-called perfection.

I can hear the detective murmuring something, so I scoot to the foot of the bed and listen. It sounds like he's repeating my requests to someone. God, I hope that someone is another agent and not my father. I hope I haven't been tricked. I hope this isn't another part of my punishment for telling Ryler my secrets.

A minute later, the agent returns to the room with a pleased smile on his face. "Emery, you have yourself a deal. Ryler is on his way and all your requests will be taken care of as soon as we have the location of the warehouse."

He waits for me to spill the biggest, most dangerous secret I ever will. My lips part to utter the name of the town, but the word weighs in my throat.

"Can I have a pen and a piece of paper?" I ask.

He nods and collects a pen and notebook from the drawer of the nightstand and hands them to me. I press the tip of the pen to the paper and my hand moves, betraying my father, my mother, all I've ever known.

Ralingford is the town you're looking for. That's where the warehouse is.

The pen falls from my hands, and finally, for the first time ever, I taste it.

Freedom.

A Life-Altering Choice.

Ryler

I'm in deep shit. That was made clear the moment three of Detective Stale's cop buddies came barging into my apartment. They woke up Violet and Luke and gave me about two minutes to explain what the fuck was going on, why I texted Stale I was about to tell Emery and run.

"I'm sorry," I signed to a horrified Luke while Greg, the taller, sturdier of Stale's cop friends urged me to get my ass out the door. Jay, the shortest of the group, had Emery in his arms, because I refused to go anywhere without her.

"Sorry for what?" Luke blinked his eyes and scanned the three men standing in our narrow, somewhat messy living room. "What the fuck is going on, man?"

Violet walked up behind him, her hair a mess, her eyes bloodshot from sleepiness. "Holy shit, what's going on?"

I debated lying to them since it was what I was supposed to do, but I had already fucked up my informant position big time the moment I sent Stale that text. Already in balls deep, I decided to just tell them everything I could.

"I've been working as an informant since before I ever moved here. In exchange for my help with the police, my criminal record was going to be wiped," I sign with urgency. "Tonight I've pretty much made a choice that I was going to quit."

Luke's gaze roams to Emery, unconscious, her head slumped back in Jay's arms. "What happened to her?"

"Well, to make a long story short, I was helping bring Emery's father down, and this was his way of punishing her for telling me his secrets." My hands were moving so fervently I'm not even sure they could interpret what I was saying. They must have understood enough, though, because both of their expressions plummeted.

Violet shuffled forward, tugging at the bottom of her worn T-shirt. "What's going to happen to you?"

I shrugged, glancing back at Greg. "I have no idea."

"Are you… are you going to be okay?"

"I don't know."

Luke stepped toward me. "Tell us what you need, man. How can we help?"

I shook my head and shrugged. "You can't. And I might not be coming back, but just know everything will be okay. And thanks for everything."

"Ryler." Violet stepped toward me with her arms stretched out.

That was when Greg intervened. "We need to go. Now."

He gave me a little push, and I stumbled toward the door, shooting Luke and Violet an apologetic look, knowing there was a chance I wasn't going to see them again.

I spend the next three days in and out of the police station, being locked up in a motel room, and getting probed with questions, watching countless television shows and movies, and eating out of a vending machine. On day two,

Stale reams into me, telling me how much I fucked up. I let him rattle on and on, even though I didn't fully agree with him. When I made my choice that I was going to tell Emery, it was a decision I felt good about.

Problem is, I haven't seen her since Detective Stale's friends dragged us out of my apartment.

"Where's Emery?" I ask Stale on day three after he enters my motel room with a kind of shocked expression on his face. "And when the fuck am I going to be let out of here? Or am I not leaving?"

"This place stinks like cigarettes and coffee," he remarks as he walks up to the foot of the bed. Bags permanently reside under his eyes, his clothes are wrinkled, and he reeks of coffee. "I told you that you couldn't leave until I figure out what we're going to do with you." He pulls out a chair at the table, sits down, and lowers his head into his hands. "You do realize how bad you've screwed up, right? That this could have gone a lot worse. Doc could have gotten to you first and you wouldn't be sitting here."

I point the remote at the television, click it off, and then sit up on the bed, stretching my arms. "I already told you I don't care," I sign when he raises his head again. "Emery didn't deserve what was happening to her, and I was sick of sitting by and watching them torture her."

He shakes his head. "What I don't get is why you think you needed to run with her? We could have gotten you out of there and then followed Doc when he took Emery home."

I lower my feet onto the floor. "Because more than likely Doc would have hurt her before he got her home."

"You don't know that for sure." His voice is harsh, but he looks worn out. "Do you have any idea what you did? You crumbled year's worth of work all so you could try and save some girl, just like you did with Aura."

"Don't bring her into this," I warn. "Emery's not Aura. She wouldn't have told her father who I am."

He heaves an exhausted breath and stares out the window. "I can't believe you blew your cover and gave up your chance at a new start in life." He looks at me and shakes his head in disappointment.

I shrug, unsure what he wants me to say. I already knew the new start I was promised is gone. I don't regret

250

my choice, though, not after seeing Evan and Doc go after Emery like that. I wasn't about to stand by and watch them slowly kill her anymore.

"I wish you'd tell me where Emery is," I sign. "It's been three days and all anyone will ever say is that she's okay, and that she's been in and out of consciousness."

"She's okay." He twists in his seat and stretches out his legs across the floor. "More than okay, actually, which is part of the reason I came to see you."

"What do you mean?"

"I mean, she finally woke up and is coherent."

I get to my feet and rub my dreary eyes, suddenly feeling very awake. "Can I see her?"

He thrums his fingers on the table, contemplating, then retrieves his phone from his pocket and checks his messages. When he puts his phone away, he reclines back in the chair. "She told us where it is."

I gape at him. "She told you where the warehouse is? Just like that?"

"You seem shocked," Stale remarks, pushing to his feet, "yet you've been assuring me that she'd cooperate."

"Yeah, but I didn't think she'd do it that easy. Not when she's terrified of her father."

"Well, she didn't do it without some stipulations, one being protection."

So, just like that, Emery gave up the location. She's braver than I thought. I should have given her more credit. All that time we spent together, she seemed timid and sweet, unlike her father who is more terrifying than the devil himself. But she's had bravery hidden beneath the fear he worked to instill in her.

"There were more requests than just being protected," Stale adds. "One is she wants to see you before she goes."

"Goes?" I ask with my brow cocked. "Where?"

"That information is confidential."

"And what about me?" I sign. "Where am I going?"

"That's really up to you." He rubs his hand over the top of his head, staring out the window again. "We can offer you witness protection, which I think would be wise considering, but I can't make you do it."

"Just like Brooks?" I question with speculation, still not convinced Brooks was ever safe.

He scowls at me. "I've told you time and time again that Brooks is safe, Ryler. Just like you and I are standing here. I told you I'd protect you just like I told him the same. We pulled him out before Donny got to him, so stop speculating otherwise."

"Why would you give me the offer for witness protection?" I wonder. "I fucked up, which means I lose my chance at starting over."

His mouth curves to a frown. "We're not that cruel. We're not going to just let you out there to fend for yourself after you've given us eight months of your life. Besides, you didn't fuck up completely. You brought us Emery who told us the location of Ralingford."

"That's the town where the warehouse is?"

"It is. Emery even gave up the latitude and longitude so we could track it by satellite, otherwise, we'd be going into the search blind."

Emery, you're more amazing than you'll ever realize.

Completely and utterly brave.

I want to see you again.

Hold you in my arms.

But how long will it last before you slip from my fingers

and blow into the wind like dust?

"And if I choose witness protection, then I'd never see anyone I know again, right?" I ask. "That would be the deal."

"That's how these things have to work; otherwise, there would be no point." When I don't respond right away, he adds, "Ryler, I'm not going to tell you what to do, but with you and Emery being gone for over four days now, my bet is Doc already has men looking for you. You know as well as I do that if they start looking into you, they're going to eventually find stuff. Just like you know that even if we arrest them there's always a chance someone will still come looking for you."

Well, when he puts it that way, it's really not a choice. Yes, it'll suck leaving my stuff behind, leaving without saying goodbye to Violet and Luke, but it's what I have to do. The worst is knowing that I won't see Emery ever again. We never really got a chance. My encounter with the beautiful girl I briefly connected to was more fleeting than a storm.

"When would I have to leave?" I ask Detective Stale. "I'm guessing soon."

"We'd get you out of here as soon as you're finished saying goodbye to Emery," he says, checking the time on his phone. "Which I'm hoping you'll make quick for her sake. A team is about to raid Ralingford, and I want her on a plane before that happens."

I rake my hands through my hair and then sniff my shirt, which smells like barbeque chips and soda. I need a shower and to put clean clothes on, but there's not a whole lot I can do since I have nothing else with me except another shirt that I wore the first two days in this room.

"Where is she?" I ask, slipping on my boots.

He heads for the door, signaling for me to follow him. "I can only give you about half an hour, then we have to get you and her out of here." He unfastens the lock, opens the door, and sticks his head out into the hallway. He glances left and right before stepping out.

I follow after him as he hurries down the hallway. We rush past door after door until finally stopping in front of the last one.

Stale slips his hand into his pocket and digs out a keycard. "Thirty minutes," he warns as he feeds the lock the card. "Then I'm coming in."

I can tell by the look on his face that he thinks Emery and I are going to spend our time fucking each other. While I don't mind the idea, I doubt that's going to happen. Things need to be said. A lot of important things, including an apology on my part for lying to her.

When Stale steps back, I push the door open and enter the room. The curtains are drawn shut and the corner lamp is on. The air smells like takeout and the bed is unmade, but Emery is nowhere to be seen.

Confused, I start across the room. As I pass by the bathroom, Emery strolls out and crashes into me.

"Oh, my God," she squeaks, pressing her hand to her heart. "You scared the heck out of me."

Her wet hair runs loosely down her shoulders, her skin is damp, and she smells like shampoo. She has on a pair of shorts and a faded black tank top. Not a single drop of makeup is on her face, and all I can think is *absolutely perfect.*

"Hey," I sign, giving her a nervous smile. Now that she knows who I am, it feels like we're meeting for the first time. And like the very first time we met, I feel a bit anxious.

"Hey," she replies, biting her nails.

I can't help smiling. She's still the same Emery.

I remove her hand from her lips and lace our fingers together. *"We need to talk,"* I mouth.

She nods in agreement. "Yes, we do."

Holding onto her hand, I guide her to the bed and pull her down with me as I sit down on the mattress. I stare at her for a while, wasting at least five of our thirty minutes together memorizing her lips, her eyes, the curves of her body, the scent of her.

"I'm sorry," I finally sign, after I finish staring at her.

Her head angles to the side. "For what?"

"For lying to you." I tuck a strand of her wet hair behind her ear. "I should have told you who I was the moment Doc told me who you were."

She burrows her cheek deeper into my hand. "Ryler, you don't need to be sorry. You're the good one here."

"I'm anything but good. Trust me."

"I do trust you." She reaches for me, her hand noticeably trembling, and sweeps her fingers through my hair. "I trust you more than anyone, which might seem crazy because we barely know each other, but I really do. I realize that now. You're the only person in my entire life that has made me feel some sort of safety. I just wish I could have trusted you from the beginning. Things would have been so much easier."

"You couldn't trust me all the time because I was lying to you most of the time."

"But you lied for a good reason."

"I should have told you who I was sooner," my hands move desperately between us, "instead of waiting until things got as bad as they did."

She lowers her hand to her lap then tucks her chin in, lowering her head. "You didn't tell me because you didn't trust me for a good reason. Who I am—where I come from—it makes me untrustworthy."

I dip my head and make eye contact with her, lifting my hands. "No, it doesn't. Just because you came from that place, it doesn't make you a monster like Elderman or your father. Trust me, if where we came from made us who we are, then I'd have no chance of starting over. I'd always be a criminal through and through, but I know I'm not. I know I want to be a good person, and one day I will be."

"You are a good person," she whispers softly. "You got me out of there—got me out of that life."

"No, you got yourself out of there by telling the truth. You're a very brave person, Emery." I smooth my finger along her jawline and fall deeper into my feelings for her as she shivers from my touch. "And don't ever think anything less."

Her tongue slides out to wet her lips as she lifts her head back up. We stare at each other in silence, the clock ticking. I don't want to move, though, because moving means moving forward. Means starting over without her.

"What do we do now?" she asks breathlessly.

I'm not sure who moves first—maybe we both move together—but suddenly, our lips slam together and clothes are being ripped off. I peel off my shirt while Emery yanks off hers. I kick off my boots, grab a condom out of my wallet, and then slip out of my jeans before climbing back onto the bed to help Emery out of her shorts. She giggles when they get stuck on her sandals and the noise is the most amazing sound I've ever heard because there's so much freedom to it.

Once I get her undressed, I lie down on the bed and she straddles my lap. I knot my fingers through her hair, drawing her to my lips. The kiss is unlike the others we've shared, carrying more passion, more freedom, more everything. I kiss her with every ounce of emotion I've kept trapped inside me, kiss her like she's feeding me air. Then, gripping her hips, I guide her down on me and thrust inside her.

She gasps from the contact, throwing her head back and arching out her chest. "This feels so amazing." Her nails scratch my chest as I rock inside her.

With each rock, I sink deeper, my skin beading with sweat. She rolls her hips and lowers her lips to mine, kissing me fervently. I don't want it to end. I tell myself that it doesn't have to. That I shouldn't have to let go of her when I only just got her.

Eventually, we both come undone. For the briefest moment, I feel so content, feel so at peace, almost forgetting that she's leaving soon and that there's a good chance I'll never see her again.

Emery lays her head on my chest right above my racing heart, still straddling me as we both work to catch our breaths .

"I don't want to leave you," she whispers, tracing circles on my chest. She tips her head, resting her chin on my chest as she peers up at me. "Not when I don't know if I'll ever see you again."

"We might one day," I sign then smooth her damp hair out of her face.

"Yeah, maybe." She remains silent, chewing on her lip, her eyes glazing over as she gets lost in thought.

"What are you thinking about?"

A faint smile touches her lips. "You're always asking me that."

"That's because you're hard to read," I sign, dropping a kiss on her lips. "And I want to know what's on your mind."

She pushes up and swings her legs off me. "You know, I used to think you asked me that because my father was making you. That he was trying to have you get into my head."

"Emery." I sit up in front of her. "I never wanted to use you. Most of the time we spent together, especially in the beginning, was real for me."

"I believe you and that's not why I'm bringing this up." She grabs a pillow and hugs it tightly against her chest. "I was just thinking how great it would be if we could run away together, but then I realized how impossible that is."

The moment the words leave her lips, the moment she puts it out there, I know I'm facing a life-altering choice.

"Why is that so impossible if we both want it?" I sign to her.

Do we both want it? Do I want it? I barely know her and she hardly knows me, yet somehow we know more about each other than others know about us. That has to mean something, right?

"You don't want it." She frowns, cuddling the pillow closer. "Trust me. You don't want me like that."

"No… I'm pretty sure I do."

She rapidly shakes her head, her eyes widening. "Ryler, you don't even know me… don't even know what you're getting into." My hands lift to protest but she continues on. "You remember at the concert how I told you that I'm crazy? Well, that's one of the few times when I was telling you the painful truth."

"You're not crazy," I insist, scooting closer to her, the mattress caving in under my weight. "You've just had a rough life."

Her eyes water with tears. "My parents had me on these pills most of my life, and I found out a month ago that those pills were for psychosis."

"Your parents are the fucking crazy ones." I snatch hold of the pillow and chuck it aside. "You need to realize that."

"I sometimes see my dead brother," she divulges, wide-eyed in horror. "I think it's out of guilt, but still… That's not normal."

I swallow the lump welling in my throat. So that's why Doc always referred to his son in the past tense. "When did he… when did he die?"

"Before I left for Laramie," she explains. "I caught my father burying him in the basement, and he threatened to kill me if I didn't help cover his death up. I somehow blocked the memory out, but then it started surfacing when I stopped taking the pills. That's when Ellis started showing up. I would talk to him and everything, but couldn't figure out why. Then I remembered *everything*." She begins to sob, heart-wrenching sounds that pierce my soul. "You need to go. Run away from me."

Some might say she's right—that I should run away and leave her. It would be the easy thing to do, just like it was easy for Aura to bail out on me when I needed her. Just like it was easy for my father and mother to bail out on me. Easy, easy, easy and my life will be perfect, perfect, perfect.

I don't want perfect, though. I don't want to let her go. Don't believe that she's as crazy as she thinks she is. She's just lost. Besides, who am I to judge her after all the shit I've done? In my own way, I'm crazy, too.

"I want to help you, Emery. Let me help you." I wipe her tears away with my fingers and pull her onto my lap.

"But I'm crazy," she whispers, her eyelashes fluttering as she blinks back the tears. "You shouldn't want to help me."

"No, I should. I really, really should because… I care about you, Emery, more than I've cared about anyone before," I sign the most honest thing I ever have in my entire life. "And honestly, everyone is crazy in their own way, depending on how you look at it."

She looks at me like I'm insane but then a laugh sputters from her lips. "Are you being serious right now?"

My lips quirk. "More serious than I've ever been."

"So, we're really going to do this?" Hope gleams in her eyes. "Go away together? Because it just seems so… Well, crazy."

I press my lips together and nod my head. "If that's the case, then I guess the choice is fitting."

She stares at me for another second or two before wrapping her arms around me, and I cling on to her, knowing that I made the right choice.

"But what about Stale?" Emery pulls back. "Is he going to allow us to do this?"

I shrug. "Doesn't really matter. We've already pretty much gone against everyone. What's one more person?"

"You're right," she agrees, then leans in to kiss me.

For a moment, everything is perfect, everything feels right. And I truly believe there's more perfection for us in the future now that Emery and I are finally free from our past. Are finally free to be ourselves and live the lives we've always wanted to, under our own freewill. Together. We won't have to go through this alone.

I kiss her back fully, cupping the back of her head and pulling her closer.

Suddenly the door creaks open. "I'm coming in in exactly one minute. If anyone needs to get dressed, better make it quick," Stale calls out, shattering the moment into pieces.

Emery and I spring from the bed and scramble to put on our clothes. By the time Stale walks in, Emery is ruffling her hair into place and I'm doing up my belt.

Stale's gaze dances back and forth between us before landing on me. "It's time to go." He looks at Emery. "You too. There's a car waiting for you outside that's going to drive you to the airport."

Emery sucks her bottom lip between her teeth and stares at me helplessly. I give her hand a squeeze before turning to Stale.

"We want to go together," I sign to him. The movement of my hands and arms are firm despite how fast my heart is racing.

Stale immediately shakes his head. "It's too risky for the two of you to go together. It'll make it easier for someone to identify you or track you down."

I nervously pop my knuckles, hesitating with what to say next. He could be right. It could be more dangerous if Emery and I go together. Do I want to put her at risk like that?

"I want to go with him," Emery chimes in. "I don't care if it's more risky." When she looks at me, her confidence sinks along with her shoulders. "Unless you've changed your mind."

"I just don't want to put you in danger," I sign, feeling like an asshole. "That's it, Emery. I want to go with you more than anything. I promise."

"Then do it." The plea in her voice rips my heart in two. "I don't care if it's more risky. I've lived my whole life doing what I thought I was supposed to, following orders, doing what everyone else wanted me to do. For once,

I just want to live my life how I want and be with the people I want." She crosses her arms, frowning. "But I get it. It's a big risk. One you shouldn't have to take."

I want to take it.

God, do I.

Say to hell with everything

and soar away.

Start a life

that I can finally live

without feeling as though I'm half dead.

"No, I want to... I want you..." My unsteady hands move in front of me.

She reaches for me and takes hold of my hands. "Then let's do this."

A breath eases from my lips as I bob my head up and down. Then I slip my hands from hers and turn to Stale who looks madder than hell. "We're going together."

He shakes his head. "I can't allow that. It's too risky."

"Then I guess we'll start over on our own." I'm not being serious. I know for a fact we can't start over under these circumstances without help. I just need him to believe that we will if he doesn't help us.

"Don't be stupid, Ryler," Stale stresses. "This is what you've always wanted—a new life. It's the reason you got into this in the first place."

Emery's brows furrow, and I realize there's still so much she doesn't know about me.

"I'll explain later," I mouth to her.

"I'm just glad there's going to be a later," she replies, looking more excited than I've ever seen her.

Stale huffs an aggravated breath and folds his arms, staring us down like a parent scolding his children. "You two have got to be kidding me. This is absurd. And we need to go before you don't have a chance of getting out of here undetected."

I don't respond. I simply take Emery's hand and interlock our fingers. My heart skips a beat when she grips on for dear life.

A minute of silence ticks by before Stale throws his hands in the air. "Fine. Do whatever you want. See if I care." He storms for the door and jerks it open. At first, I think he's really going to leave and let us do this on our own, but then he shoots us an impatient look. "Are you two coming?"

I suppress a grin as I nod, then Emery and I walk to the door. We don't take anything with us, except the clothes on our backs and each other. It makes me feel weightless and, in the strangest way, happy.

As I step over the threshold, I smile to myself because I can almost feel myself entering a new life, the one I've always wanted.

I'm finally, finally free.

Chapter 19

I Finally Found My Wings

Eight months later…

Emery

"So, you're saying you think the reason why I forgot so many things about my life is because of the medication I was on?" I ask my therapist, a middle-aged woman with wild red hair. "That it was a side effect?"

She crosses her arms on top of her cluttered desk. "It could be because of a side effect. Although, if the right person knew a lot about the drug, they might administer it in an attempt to give a person temporary amnesia."

I sigh heavily. "It's probably the latter."

She hesitates, chewing on the end of her pen. "I know you've said that you don't want to tell me who was giving you the drugs all those years, but I want to remind you that you can trust me." She motions at the closed door. "Every-thing that gets said in here is strictly confidential, Em."

She calls me Em and believes my name is Emelia, just like everyone else I meet does. It's the name I was given eight months ago when I was relocated to Florida under witness protection.

I thrum my fingers on the armrests. I would love to tell her everything, but doing so would be risking my new iden-tity, and right now, it's not worth the risk.

"I'll keep that in mind," I finally say.

"All right then." She sifts through a file on the desk, moving on. "So, how are the hallucinations coming along? Have you had any?"

I shake my head. "Not for quite a few months."

"That's good." She jots something down on a legal pad. "That makes me believe even more that they were stemming from the medication you were on. Although, I do believe that you saw your brother as a coping mechanism over the guilt you felt because of his death."

I nod, almost agreeing with her this time. In the beginning, I was so caught up in the madness that it was hard for me to believe the drugs were causing my mind to slip away.

I haven't seen Ellis since the day I remembered his death, so I'm hoping she's right. Still, life hasn't been easy. I do have nightmares at least once a week and my panic attacks can get intense. But that's part of life. Even Ryler has stuff he's dealing with, like missing Violet and Luke and sometimes he sinks into a funk. But we're always there to help each other out.

"What about your anxiety?" she asks.

I shrug. "It comes and goes."

She scrawls down something else. "Good. You're doing really well. You've made great progress over the last several months." She sets down the pen and paper. "I'm proud of you."

I offer her a small smile. "Thanks." My attention drifts to the clock on the wall. "Oh, shit, I'm going to be late." I spring from the chair and reach for my bag on the floor.

She pushes back from her desk. "Late for what? I thought you didn't have class today."

"I don't." I walk backward toward the door. "I'm meeting someone, though."

She smiles as she walks back to the filing cabinet and puts my folder away. "Have fun with Reece. I'll see you next Tuesday."

"How do you know I'm meeting Ryl—Reece?" I ask as I turn the doorknob, cringing when I almost call Ryler by his real name.

Sometimes it happens, and it probably doesn't help that when we're behind closed doors, we still call each other Emery and Ryler. He'll always be Ryler to me, the first guy I ever trusted and felt love for.

"Because you only ever smile like that when you're meeting him." She shuts the filing cabinet drawer. "Go have fun, Em. You deserve it."

Throwing a wave over my shoulder, I hurry down the hallway of the University of Florida where my therapy sessions take place and where I attend school. It's the end of fall semester, and the hall is buzzing with energy as finals wrap up. Soon, the holidays will be here and everyone will clear out to go home.

Ryler and I have other plans that involve simply cuddling up at home, and I'm okay with that. More than okay, actually. Simple is good. Simple is perfection.

The hot Florida sun glistens down on me as I race across the campus lawn toward the parking lot like a mad woman, ignoring the alarmed stares thrown in my direction. After everything I've been through, getting looked at like I'm crazy doesn't matter as much anymore.

Sure, it gets to me sometimes. It was really hard when my therapist put me on a mood stabilizer, not because I have psychosis, but to help with the trauma I endured.

"Sorry, sorry, sorry," I apologize as I approach Ryler's beat up Dodge Challenger. He had to leave his old one behind, but he managed to save up and buy a junker. "Izzy and I got caught up in our session today."

Ryler is lying on the hood of his car, writing down something in his journal, looking as sexy as ever, even in faded grey shorts and a black T-shirt. "I love how you call your therapist by her first name." He closes his journal, sits up, and stretches his arms above his head.

My heart pitter-patters inside my chest as his shirt rides up. "She told me I should."

He grins when he notices me checking him out and lifts his shirt up to tease me a little. "Like what you see?" he signs, tucking his journal under his arm.

I roll my eyes, but grin as I round the car to the passenger side. "So, where are we going today?" I tug my short brown and purple hair into a ponytail and secure it with an elastic.

He slides off the hood and rakes his hands over his short black hair, a look we're still getting used to. "I was thinking we could drive down to the beach and build a sand castle. You haven't done that before. And I was thinking that we could maybe do that memorial for your brother while we're there. I mean, if you're ready. You don't have to, though. No pressure."

My brother's body is buried back in Wyoming, in a cemetery near the foothills. My mother and father were in jail, but from what I understand, no one attended the funeral. I wanted to, but Detective Stale warned that going back to Laramie would be risking my new life. Even though I still feel horrible over it, I decided it was best not to go.

But I've been meaning to do something in his memory, and Ryler suggested I write a letter to him that we can stick in a bottle and send out to sea. That way it lives on for as long as the water will carry it.

I suck in a deep breath. "No, I'm ready to do it. It's time to say goodbye I think."

He nods then his lips tug into a devious grin. "And I brought Jäger for afterward, so we can spend the rest of the night calling each other pretty."

Even after eight months, I still get the slightest bit embarrassed over my drunken words. I shake my head, my cheeks warming, but then I laugh. "Good. Can't wait."

A long time ago, when Ryler and I first met, he promised to give me a lot of firsts. He's been making good on that promise since we got here. Every free day we get from our classes and jobs, we spend time doing stuff. He started with all the intimate stuff first; teaching me things about sex, my body, and myself that I didn't know even existed. Then came the everyday stuff, like driving a stick shift, trying new foods, watching movies I'd never seen before, see-ing the ocean for the first time. I even got my very first tattoo; an intricate tree that weaves up my shoulders blades, the branches shifting into birds at the base of my neck. With each prick of the needle, I felt freer and freer from my old life, and Ryler was there to hold my hand.

I'm so different from the girl who grew up in Raling-ford, and I'd like to believe that if anyone from my old life ever saw me, they wouldn't recognize who I am. I hope that's the case.

Even though Donny Elderman, my father, my mother, and a lot of others were arrested when Ralingford was brought down, some managed to escape. While I'm not positive my father won't have someone track me down, all I can do is live my life. All I can do is keep breathing and be grateful that I have the freedom to breathe.

"And thank you," I tell him. "I really mean it. Thank you for everything. For being there for me when no one else has ever been."

He smiles warmly. "I'll always be there for you, Em. You should know that by now."

"I do." Smiling, I climb in the car.

He opens the driver's side door, slides into the seat, and turns on the engine. "You look happy," he signs with a thoughtful look on his face, then tugs at a loose strand of my hair.

"I am happy," I reply, buckling my seatbelt.

"Good. I want you to be happy."

"I want you to be happy, too."

"I am," he mouths. Then just to prove his point, he leans over the console and kisses me with so much passion I damn near melt into a puddle on his seat. When he pulls away, he flashes me a lopsided grin and backs the car out of the parking spot.

I pick up the iPod, turn on "The Drug In Me Is You" by Falling In Reverse, and hum along to the lyrics.

As Ryler drives out onto the road, he laces our fingers together, and I grip on tight. My heart flutters with excitement like it does every time I'm with him. I love that it's able to react that way. Love that my past didn't ruin me completely.

During the beginning of our move, I worried I was broken. That I'd never be normal. And while I don't believe that I completely fit the definition now, I'm content with where I am. Normal is overrated anyway. Being yourself is what's most important. And I finally found who that is—who I am.

We hold hands for most of the drive. By the time we make it to the shoreline, the sun is descending and the sky above the water shimmers with hues of pink and gold.

Ryler and I get out of the car with a bottle and the letter I wrote and hike down the beach to where the ocean kisses the shore.

I stand in the sand, staring out at the lulling water, the wind blowing through my hair. "Ellis never got to see the ocean," I say softly, my heart fluttering in my chest.

This is harder than I thought.

But saying goodbye is always difficult.

Ryler squeezes my hand, and the contact gives me the strength I need.

I give one final glance at the paper, skimming over the words I wrote to Ellis.

You were the best brother I never really got to know.

The brother who came to me after death

and forgave me for forgetting

things that should have never been forgotten.

I wish I could have given you more.

Saved you before the dirt took you.

Saved you from being smothered

by the man who gave us air.

Saved you from everything.

I wish you could have seen

how great the world could be,

if you soared high above the life we knew

and flew away into the clouds.

I wish that you could have found your wings.

I'm sorry you never did.

I'll try my best to fly high for the both of us.

Live the life we should have always had.

Goodbye, Ellis.

I hope one day I'll see you again.

With a deep breath, I roll up the paper and stuff it into the bottle. Then I put the cork into the top and walk forward until the water rolls over my feet.

"Goodbye," I whisper then chuck the bottle toward the waves, watching it fly away.

I keep my eyes on it as it bobs up and down, finally disappearing out of my sight.

Ryler joins me, twining our fingers together. He leans forward and mouths, *"Are you okay?"*

I nod, grip onto him tight, and stand on my tiptoes to kiss him. "You know what? I really think I am," I tell him when I move back.

And it's the truth.

Because for the first time ever, it feels like I've finally found my wings.

About the Author

Jessica Sorensen is a *New York Times* and *USA Today* bestselling author that lives in the snowy mountains of Wyoming. When she's not writing, she spends her time reading and hanging out with her family.

Other books by Jessica Sorensen:

<u>The Coincidence Series:</u>

    The Coincidence of Callie and Kayden

    The Redemption of Callie and Kayden

    The Destiny of Violet and Luke

    The Probability of Violet and Luke

    The Certainty of Violet and Luke

    The Resolution of Callie and Kayden

    Seth & Grayson (Coming Soon)

The Secret Series:

The Prelude of Ella and Micha

The Secret of Ella and Micha

The Forever of Ella and Micha

The Temptation of Lila and Ethan

The Ever After of Ella and Micha

Lila and Ethan: Forever and Always

Ella and Micha: Infinitely and Always

The Shattered Promises Series:

Shattered Promises

Fractured Souls

Unbroken

Broken Visions

Scattered Ashes (Coming Soon)

Breaking Nova Series:

Breaking Nova

Saving Quinton

Delilah: The Making of Red

Nova and Quinton: No Regrets

Tristan: Finding Hope

Wreck Me

Ruin Me

The Fallen Star Series (YA):

The Fallen Star

The Underworld

The Vision

The Promise

The Fallen Souls Series (spin off from The Fallen Star):

The Lost Soul

The Evanescence

The Darkness Falls Series:

Darkness Falls

Darkness Breaks

Darkness Fades

The Death Collectors Series (NA and YA):

Ember X and Ember

Cinder X and Cinder

Spark X and Cinder (Coming Soon)

The Sins Series:

Seduction & Temptation

Sins & Secrets

Unbeautiful Series:

Unbeautiful

Untamed

Unraveling Series:

Unraveling You

Raveling You

Awakening You

Standalones

The Forgotten Girl

Coming Soon:

Entranced

Steel & Bones

Connect with me online:

jessicasorensen.com

http://www.facebook.com/pages/Jessica-Sorensen/165335743524509

https://twitter.com/#!/jessFallenStar

Untamed